THE
FOUNDATION DECISION

(THE FINAL CHAPTER OF THE DIABOLICAL TRILOGY)

D. PATRICK CARROLL

PublishAmerica
Baltimore

© 2013 by D. Patrick Carroll.
All rights reserved. No part of this book may be reproduced, stored in a retrieval system or transmitted in any form or by any means without the prior written permission of the publishers, except by a reviewer who may quote brief passages in a review to be printed in a newspaper, magazine or journal.

First printing

All characters in this book are fictitious, and any resemblance to real persons, living or dead, is coincidental.

PublishAmerica has allowed this work to remain exactly as the author intended, verbatim, without editorial input.

Softcover 9781629071824
PUBLISHED BY PUBLISHAMERICA, LLLP
www.publishamerica.com
Baltimore

Printed in the United States of America

Dedicated to; My older brother Dave Armstrong, who has been a general pain in my butt, and I love dearly.

Dave —
Enough Said
Hope you enjoy

Cet ouvrage a été composé en Caslon par Palimpseste à Paris

Achevé d'imprimer en février 2003
sur presse Cameron
dans les ateliers de
Bussière Camedan Imprimeries
à Saint-Amand-Montrond (Cher)
pour le compte de la librairie Arthème Fayard
75, rue des Saints-Pères - 75006 Paris

35-67-1695-2/01

ISBN 2-213-61495-4

Dépôt légal : février 2003.
N° d'Édition : 29707. – N° d'Impression : 030597/4.

Imprimé en France

AUTHOR'S INTRODUCTION

For those readers who have not read my two previous books of this trilogy ('Diabolical' and 'El Diablo y Los Santos') and to avoid redundancy for those who have, and because I'm a lazy author, the following gives a brief description of some of the primary characters I have brought into 'The Foundation Decision':

Charles 'Chuck' Chalmers: Former Senior Homicide Inspector with the San Francisco Police Department, retired. He's fifty-six years old (or is it fifty-seven, he can't remember) and a husband and father of three, two grown sons and a daughter in high school. In 'Diabolical' he was the lead detective investigating a serial murderer that went unsolved. He was subsequently, after his retirement from the force, (read the book) kind of suckered into participating with a group of very rich people to hunt down and bring the serial murderer to justice. He is a dedicated investigator in pursuit of justice and a loving and caring husband and father who has come to grips with his midlife crisis after retirement and appreciates his family for tolerating his indulgences.

Colleen Chalmers: Loving and beautiful wife of Chuck. She's about four or five (he can't remember) years younger than himself. She's willing to sacrifice her idea of retired life and although sometimes reluctantly, tolerates Chuck's indulgences.

Jennifer Chalmers: The loving daughter of Chuck and Colleen. She's sixteen now and a junior in high school. She has a keen mind and a wit to match. She tragically lost her best friend, Tracy Barnes (read 'El Diablo y Los Santos') when the Barnes family was brutally murdered. She admires her father, but is not above using circumstances to her advantage. Her mother has described her as a 'devious little imp'.

Mary Dinosa: Former homicide inspector and partner of Chalmers'. She's beautiful, thirty-one years old and would self-describe herself as a 'feisty bitch'. She has a mouth that would 'embarrass a long shore man in a whorehouse'. Despite her creative vocabulary, she is well respected by her peers and has resigned her position with the SFPD to accept a position as a Special Investigator with the Justice Department. Since participating in one of Chalmers' covert missions, she has now come to terms with when breaking the law justifies the end.

Valerie Kane: She's another beautiful feisty lady approaching fifty years old. As an Assistant District Attorney for the county and city of San Francisco, she made up the legal arm of the task force put together to investigate and prosecute the serial murderer in 'Diabolical'. She has subsequently taken a position as a prosecutor with the U.S. Department of Justice and was instrumental in bringing Dinosa on board as her lead Investigator. She's responsible for tying together all of the legal evidence and prosecuting members of a vast conspiracy in 'El Diablo y Los Santos'.

Sean O'Farrell: Heir to the vast O'Farrell fortune. He's a fifth generation San Francisco native whose ancestor, Joseph

O'Farrell landed in San Francisco and started a mercantile business catering to the gold miners and pioneers in 1848. He is the husband of one of the victims of serial killer George Spinella, pursued and apprehended in 'Diabolical', and one of the founding members of what would become the 'Justice Foundation'. His guarded and fortified estate in Sausalito, California, has become the sanctuary for foundation team members and their families during team operations.

Ian O'Farrell: Son of Sean and heir apparent to the O'Farrell family fortune. He's a former U.S. Navy Seal team Commander who resigned his commission shortly after his mother was murdered. He had become disenchanted with the political agenda and aspirations that had pervaded military operations. His new mission became avenging his mother's death and in 'Diabolical' he assembles former loyal members of his Seal team and joins with Chuck Chalmers to pursue and capture the infamous George Spinella, the serial killer that murdered his mother. The team remains together and becomes the field operational team for the Foundation. At the end of 'El Diablo y Los Santos' he becomes romantically involved with Mary Dinosa.

Sheila Lamont-O'Farrell: Daughter of Sean and oldest sibling. Her husband was an Army Special Forces soldier who was killed in Afghanistan several years ago. She has returned to the O'Farrell Estate after her mother was murdered to become the family Matriarch. She has two children, sixteen year old Shannon who has become good friends with Jennifer Chalmers and eighteen year old Matthew who has become infatuated with Jennifer Chalmers.

Solomon Goldsmith: Husband of George Spinella's first victim. Among other businesses he owns is a company called 'S and G Imports'. That company owns the exclusive rights to import and distribute in the United States several popular foreign beer brands. He's responsible for gathering together other family members who are also survivors of Spinella's victims and forming what would become the 'Justice Foundation'.

George Armstrong: The son of Helen Armstrong, Spinella's fourth victim and one of the heirs to the Armstrong Publishing Empire. He is a practicing criminal defense lawyer and a board member of the 'Justice Foundation'. He's a highly intelligent man and one of the operation planners.

Steve and Nancy Cromwell, Grant Wilson and Jesse Leone: Former members of the Seal team commanded by Ian O'Farrell, they are loyal field operatives dedicated to carrying out the 'Justice Foundation" decisions. Steve and Nancy have moved on and invested in a small ski resort in northern California. They remain 'on-call'.

Daniel and Belinda Tanaka: Belinda, better known as Snoops or Snoopy, was an IT on the Computer Forensic Unit with the SFPD and worked with the task force investigating the serial murderer in Diabolical. She met Daniel, preferred to be called Grub, when the 'Foundation' recruited him to conduct electronic surveillance among other things. He's known as the top dog in the computer hacking business. It was love at first byte and they were married in the last book.

Bernard Rusk: Aka 'Los Santos', is a true American patriot. He started his career in the Nation's Capital as a young and naïve field agent with the CIA and participated in black ops during the Viet Nam War. After the war he returned to civilian life to pursue a career as a criminal defense attorney and a part time law professor at the Harvard School of Law when he first met and tutored a young law student, Valerie Kane. He was subsequently lured back to Washington, D.C. by his former boss at the CIA and became an analyst for the Agency. He became a member of an elite and secretive society within the CIA that gathered information and dossiers on corrupt politicians and other power driven individuals that he and other members believed to be a threat to the national security. He subsequently learned about the 'Justice Foundation' and the involvement of his old friend George Armstrong and their successful missions in 'Diabolical' an 'El Diablo y Los Santos'. He stood by as a silent admirer and when he was approached by a former law student, Valerie Kane, he provided logistical and operational assistance in an attempt to uncover a vast conspiracy. Valerie Kane came to realize this unassuming figure yielded much more power that she had previously thought.

This is beginning to read like a bad soap opera (and to some it might well be), but for now, study and remember these characters (you will be tested later) and join them as they journey into another 'Foundation Decision'.

PART I

THE WAR

"There are no winners in war, only losers. When the final toll is taken, the only good result is it is over." Author Unknown, but the thought of many who fought

CHAPTER ONE

Solomon Goldsmith stood at the entrance to B'nai B'rith Synagogue, better known as the House of Hosea, shaking hands with Rabbi David Began. It was an early San Francisco Fall evening and the traffic on Geary Street was light after the Saturday service.

"Sol, it's so good to see you," the Rabbi said.

"It's good to see you too, Rabbi."

"I was hoping you could stay for a while. There's something I'd like to discuss with you," Began said, releasing his grip.

"I'm sorry David, but I have a sick mother at home and I should be getting along. Sorry, I'll call you later, shalom," Goldsmith said, starting towards the steps leading to the sidewalk.

The Rabbi reached under his robe and retrieved an envelope and grabbing Goldsmith by his arm he said, "Here, read this and we'll talk later."

Goldsmith stuffed the envelope in his breast pocket and hurried to the sidewalk where he felt obligated to briefly acknowledge fellow worshippers gathered and mingling in small clusters outside the synagogue.

He finally reached his car and pulled out of the parking lot next to the synagogue and made a right turn onto Geary Street. He had traveled about half a block when his car shook violently followed immediately by an ear shattering boom.

He instinctively stopped his car in the middle of the street, exited and started sprinting back toward the synagogue. Above the ringing in his ears he could hear the blaring of car alarm horns coming from all directions.

As he approached the synagogue he realized a bomb had detonated and his congregation and Synagogue was the target. Smoke and dust filled the air and as it settled and dissipated, bodies and carnage laid all about him. The Synagogue looked like a building he had seen in film clips shot after bombing air raids. Little was left of the once grand structure. The surrounding buildings sustained exterior damage and windows were shattered.

The cars parked directly in front had been hurled into the street causing a massive entanglement with passing vehicles and created a traffic jam in both directions. The friends he had just passed on the sidewalk were either unrecognizable or had disappeared. Peering into the trees that lined the street he saw body parts stuck to or hanging from now leafless and broken limbs.

In shock and disbelief he climbed the steps and tried to clear the debris to what once was the entrance to the Synagogue. A strong hand grasped his arm and pulled him back down and away from the building.

"Sir, you have to get away from the building. Please come with me," a uniformed police officer was saying from what seemed like a universe away.

Goldsmith was covered with a layer of dust and he looked blankly into the eyes of the policeman.

"Are you okay, sir? Are you injured? Is there anything I can do for you?" The officer asked sincerely.

Goldsmith just shook his head to answer no. The officer led him several buildings down and helped him sit down on the lawn of a walled front yard.

"Did you see anything?" the officer asked.

"No, no I had just left the Sabbath service and I was driving away," Goldsmith heard himself saying in what sounded like an echo above the ringing in his ears.

"Sir, can I get your name?"

Goldsmith found himself looking up at the policeman who now holding a pen and tablet.

"Huh?"

"Your name sir, can I get your name?"

"Oh, yeah, sure, it's Solomon Goldsmith." He was drifting as if he was outside of his body.

"How about your address?"

Goldsmith shook his head and suddenly he was himself again and the ringing had subsided to a low hum. He looked again at the policeman and noticed he was just a kid, no more than twenty-one or two. He became aware of his surroundings. The air was now filled with the sounds of sirens as ambulances, fire trucks and police cars converged on the scene. He gave the young officer his address.

"Sir, I've got to go see what I can do. You stay here and I'll send an EMT as soon as I can to check you out."

"That won't be necessary. I'm fine. Go tend to the others."

He watched as residents and workers stumbled shocked and dazed out onto the sidewalks from nearby buildings. Firemen and EMTs loaded bodies onto stretchers and into the backs of waiting ambulances. Others were giving aid to people lying on the ground.

He realized his car was still parked and undoubtedly blocking the intersection. He rose and trotted to where his car had been. It wasn't there. He looked frantically around and finally spotted it. Someone had driven it off Geary Street and double parked it on a side street. He got in and drove the back streets west until he could safely double back to Geary and made his way the Pacific Highway that would take him to his Cliff House Avenue home.

He opened the door to his home and was greeted by his mother shuffling behind a walker down the hall towards him.

"Oh Solomon, I was so worried about you. It's all over the news. Something terrible has happened at the Synagogue."

"I'm fine, Mom."

As she neared him and saw his condition she raised her hand to her mouth and cried, "Oh my God, look at you. Are you sure you're okay?"

"I'm fine, Mom, really. Let's get you back in the living room and let me clean up and I'll tell you all about it."

He escorted his mother back to the living room and helped her into her recliner. The news was blaring from the television and the screen was filled with a helicopter view of the carnage below.

"...We're being told that agents from Home Land Security, the FBI and the ATF are already at the scene. The death toll has reached one hundred fifty-eight with many more in critical condition and not expected to survive. Mayor Ed Bradford has called a press conference in the chambers of the city council a half hour from now and it is reported Governor Diane Wainwright is in route from Sacramento..."

"It'll be all right, Mom," Goldsmith lied, reassuringly placing a hand on each of her shoulders and squeezing them gently. "I'm going to clean myself up and I'll be back soon."

He wandered out of the room and down the hall and into his bedroom and turned on the overhead light. He caught a glance of himself in a full length mirror and coiled back. Oh my God, he thought. A Hollywood make-up artist couldn't have done a better job of creating a walking zombie. Sweat and tears had streaked down his now mud caked face and his black suit and yarmulke were now an ash gray.

He removed his skull cap and laid it on a chair and while removing his jacket he felt the envelope in the breast pocket.

"Oh shit," he whispered. He'd forgotten about the envelope Rabbi David had given to him. They were to discuss it later this evening.

He now examined the envelope for the first time. The outside was marked simply 'Jude'.

A feeling of deep dread came over him as he withdrew the letter and began to read:

To: The murderers of our Jesus and to the niggers who defile our daughters and to the mongrel Muslims who murder the innocents:

Accept this as a Declaration of Holy War against you and any who stands with you. We will destroy your synagogues and temples and churches and anywhere and anyone who stands against us. Our God and our great White Nation will prevail.

From: the 'Great White Nation'

"Chuck, its Sean. Have you been watching the news?" the senior O'Farrell said into the phone.

"Yeah, we're all crowded around the big screen in the main lodge. I've been trying to get through to you but all communication into the city has shut down. I've had the same problem trying to get a hold of Sol or George. Even Mary can't get anyone.

"We're all packed and ready to travel back to the city. What's the situation there?"

"Besides my family and Mary, who else from the team is with you?" Sean asked.

"Jesse Leone and Grant Wilson just arrived this morning along with Grub and Snoopy. Other than John Garcia we're all here," Chalmers replied and added, "What's your assessment there?"

"It's not good, Chuck. I just got off the phone with Sol. Apparently its only outside the area incoming calls that are jammed up. He gave me some very disturbing news and I've called for a board meeting. He and George will be here in the morning," Sean said.

"We're on our way," Chalmers exclaimed.

"Chuck, I think it best if only the team members come. Leave your families and let them enjoy their holiday," Sean requested.

"That may be easier said than done, but in any case, expect to see us in seven to eight hours," Chalmers responded and hung up.

Steve and Nancy Cromwell had invited some friends and fellow team members of the 'Justice Foundation' and their families to spend a few days over the Christmas break at their recently purchased ski resort located at the base of Mount Lassen in northeast corner of California. Among the guests were Chuck Chalmers, retired homicide inspector with the San Francisco Police Department, and his wife Colleen and their sixteen year old daughter Jennifer.

Ian Armstrong, former commander of the Navy Seal team that Steve and Nancy had served with, was there along with his date, Mary Dinosa, Special Investigator with the U.S. Justice Department assigned to the San Francisco district.

Ian's sister Sheila Lamont and her two children, sixteen year old Shannon and seventeen year old Matthew were also partaking of the Cromwell's hospitality. Grant and Jesse, also members of Ian's former Seal team, had arrived that morning and the entire group enjoyed the day skiing the slopes of the 'Obsidian Ski Resort'.

As they straggled in after their last ski runs of the day they assembled in the main lodge and one by one gathered around the television to watch the horrific events as they unfolded in San Francisco.

—

CHAPTER TWO

The African American male exited the bus at Leonard Avenue and West 124th Street in the Harlem District in Upper Manhattan. He was a large man and wore a white ihram that draped his body from his neck to his sandal shod feet. On his head he wore a traditional knitted kafi. Under his left arm he carried a mehrab, the traditional Muslim prayer rug.

He strolled across the street and half a block down to the entrance of an Islamic Mosque and started up the steps. Flanked on either side of the open doors stood two black men dressed in dark suits, their hands clasped together in front of them.

As he approached the doors one of the men in black stepped forward and said, "Welcome, you are not a regular worshipper here?" he asked.

"No Brother, I'm from St. Louis and on a holy pilgrimage to Mecca. My flight leaves tomorrow morning and I'm here for the evening prayer and to ask Allah for a safe passage."

The man stepped back and said, "Welcome Brother."

The large man bowed his head in submission and entered the Mosque. He found himself in a foyer. In front of him was an archway that led to a large domed room. Before him several hundred men knelt at the end of their prayer rugs.

He sprawled his rug down at the rear of the room and knelt. Suddenly a booming voice came from the front of the room. It was in a language the large black man didn't understand. The other men repeated the utterance and then bowed down with their foreheads on the floor, arms outstretched and palms down. He mimicked their actions.

When everyone returned to the upright position, the voice in front sang out again praises to Allah. As the others repeated those words, the large man unbuttoned and reached beneath his ihram and produced an automatic rifle with a fold out stock and a cylinder ammunition clip attached.

As the other men bowed he stood up and yelled, "Allah is blasphemous!" and opened fire. He aimed first at the men closest to him and spread his shots outward killing and wounding dozens. He turned toward the archway where the two men in black suits appeared with hand guns drawn. He shot both men and then returned his attention to the worshippers.

Screams shrilled out and panic filled the room, as some of the men ran for exits and some ran at the shooter. He released the cylinder clip and attached another. Backing up toward the archway he continued to mow down those rushing toward him. When he had eliminated this threat he calmly walked back through the archway and across the foyer to the outside steps.

One of the men in black followed him crawling and leaving a trail of blood.

The large black man stood at the entrance to the Mosque and with his rifle at his side started yelling, "Yea, though I walk through the valley of the shadow of death, I will fear no evil, for thou art with me..."

The back of his head exploded at the top of his spine and his forehead disappeared with bone and brains into the cool New York air as the large black man crumpled dead onto the steps. The shot came from the man in black as he took his final breath lying face down below the archway.

—

"Welcome everybody," Sean O'Farrell said with the 'Justice Foundation' members gathered together in his den. "Solomon couldn't be here this morning. He thought he would be better served tending to the needs of the survivors of his congregation. He said he'd join us later today."

He went on, "You've all been given a copy of the letter that was delivered to Rabbi David Began we believe sometime yesterday and given to Sol last evening. The original has been turned over to the FBI."

"Excuse me, Sean," Chalmers said and continued, "but his letter sounds like it came from a fanatic individual or group. As disgusting as they are, these are usually idle threats aimed at rattling cages and promoting fear. We received and investigated these threats all the time when I was with the SFPD. Is there any evidence besides coincidence that ties this letter and the people who sent it to the Synagogue bombing?"

"None yet," George Armstrong said. "My concern is, none of my resources have ever heard of this 'Great White Nation' nor can they connect it with this travesty, but some of us have already discussed the growing national problem of internal hate group fanatical terrorism and what the 'Foundations' could do about it."

"Regardless if this group had any involvement with this incident, Sol tells us the planning and execution had to be accomplished by someone or some group that was well organized and prepared. He serves on the synagogue's board of elders and says they were extremely security conscious. The temple was never left unattended by security people so planting and detonating a bomb on the premises would require expert planning," Sean said.

"That said," Armstrong interjected, "we thought it appropriate to gather the team on a stand-by status until we decide what, if anything, we can do."

"I know most of you must be exhausted. Get some rest and we'll meet later this afternoon. In the meantime, contact anyone you can think of who might contribute to our investigation," Sean said, ending the meeting.

—

"Hey Mary, thanks for meeting me on such short notice," Chalmers said as he pulled out a chair in the corner table inside Lefty's Tavern. For the past several years the tavern had served as a meeting place for the two when Chalmers needed information from his friend and former homicide partner and now a Special Investigator with the U.S. Justice Department.

"Ah, Jesus Chalmers, first name again? I'm getting that 'sacrificial virgin' feeling again. Whatcha need?" Mary Dinosa groaned.

"You know perfectly well what I need, Dinosa," Chalmers replied, with emphases on Dinosa.

"Whew, that's better. Well, after Ian dropped me off this morning I went directly to the Federal Building. My department was a zoo. Poor Valerie is up to her ass with pretrial preparation for the bastards we busted in that 'Save the World Investment' scandal. Her entire staff, including me, is working tirelessly on this shit.

"I was able to break away for a bit. Those asshole fibbies (her word for FBI Agents) are pretty tight lipped about the bombing, but I was able to find out the bomb was placed in the basement boiler room and detonated by a digital timer.

"It seems some official looking maintenance guy with City credentials showed up the day before and convinced them it was time for their annual boiler safety inspection. Other than they're frantically trying to track this guy down, that's all I know."

Chalmers stood to go and said, "Thanks Dinosa, and from what I hear you wouldn't qualify for the 'sacrificial virgin' role."

"Fuck you Chalmers."

—

"Valerie, its Bernard Rusk. I know you must be busier that an eight teeted sow with a litter of twelve, but I have a quick favor to ask," he said into the phone.

Valerie Kane, strikingly pretty, former blond now a natural brunette, is a hard hitting Federal Prosecutor. Adversaries often underestimated her 'innocent' look, but soon realized they're up against an intelligent, formidable foe.

Bernard Rusk was an old friend and her college mentor and professor when she attended Harvard Law School. Until recently she thought he was now working for the CIA as a senior analyst, but when she asked for his advice and help during the 'SWI' (Save the World Investments) investigation, she learned he yielded much more influence and power in the Nation's Capital than she previously thought.

"You have such a way with words and such a beautiful analogy, Professor. How could I refuse," Valerie Kane said sarcastically.

Bernard chuckled and said, "Well, I'm at Dulles Airport preparing to board a flight to San Francisco and I have need to meet with your friends. I was wondering if you could give me George Armstrong's number?"

Kane thought for a moment and trusting it could do no harm and since he didn't need her help to obtain Armstrong's number and sensing more favors were forthcoming, she gave him the number.

"Anything else?" she anticipated.

"How's that pistol investigator Mary Dinosa doing?" he asked.

Here it comes, Kane thought.

"I was wondering if I could borrow her for a few days during my stay there," Rusk said.

"Jesus Christ, Bernie! I'm up to my eye balls here and she's my best investigator," Kane moaned.

"Well, if it's too much to ask for…" Bernard said and then hesitated.

"Ah shit…alright, sure, okay."

"Thanks Val. Have her pick me up in front of terminal 'D' at three thirty this afternoon, will you?"

"Yes, Professor," she said hanging up.

—

Rusk threw his bag in the back of Dinosa's Subaru Outback and crawled into the passenger seat.

"Mary, so good to see you and thanks for the ride," he said cheerily taking off the Redskins ball cap that revealed his thinning grey hair.

"Nice to see you too, Mr. Rusk," Dinosa said and continued, "What are you doing flying commercial? I thought people in your position would be ferried around in one of those fancy private jets and have a limo and driver waiting for you."

"Frankly, Mary, I'm trying to stay incognito on this trip and I have a reason for requesting you," he replied.

"And what's that?" Dinosa asked skeptically as she pulled out into traffic.

"I'll fill you in when I brief the rest of the group, but I'd like you involved and act as my eyes and ears out here."

"Ah, the mystery begins. Who's the rest of the group?"

"The 'Justice Foundation', of course. I know you're one of the few people familiar with them. We're headed to my good friend George Armstrong's home now," Rusk said with a snicker.

"I've never been to his house. You'll have to give me directions," Dinosa said.

"No problem, just head south on the Bay Shore Freeway."

A drizzle of rain fell as they negotiated the route to the hills of Los Gatos and the Armstrong estate. They made small talk about the weather and that the Forty Niners and Redskins may play each other for the NFC Championship game, the winner going on to play in the Super Bowl.

When they approached the gate leading to the Armstrong place Dinosa slowed and rolled her window down. Before she could come to a complete stop the gate opened and she proceeded up the tree lined lane.

When they rounded a turn and the home came into view Dinosa was stunned.

"Holy shit," she exclaimed, "if the O'Farrell place is a mansion this must be the castle."

When they pulled into the circular driveway below the manor they were greeted by George and Ian O'Farrell. After hugs and handshakes George and Bernard started up the steps to the home's entrance, Ian and Mary following arm in arm.

In the den they met Sol, Chalmers and Sean relaxing in easy chairs. They rose and George introduced them to Bernard Rusk as their inside capital man.

George and Bernard had met some twenty years ago when they successfully represented two co-defendants falsely charged with kidnapping, rape and murder. They had made an instant bond and their friendship had grown over the ensuing years.

When they were all settled, Armstrong began, "We all know how instrumental Bernie was in bringing those involved with the 'SWI' scandal to justice. I called him yesterday thinking I'd tap his insight into the bombing of the synagogue and if he had any knowledge of this 'Great White Nation'."

"The bastard immediately cut me off and said he couldn't discuss it over the phone and we had to meet. Too many years playing James Bond, I think. Anyway, I invited him to join us and here he is. Now, you know everything I know. Go ahead, professor."

"Firstly," Rusk began, "I'd like to say I'm honored that a group such as yourselves would trust your confidence in me so let me return that confidence. Actually, I've known of your existence since your first operation to capture George Spinella. I can't reveal how I know, and it doesn't really matter anyhow, the main thing is a few of us know about you and we hold a deep respect and appreciation for what you're doing.

"I'm sure you've heard about the massacre that occurred last evening at the Muslim Mosque in New York City. At first we believed it was perpetrated by some radical Muslim faction that disagreed with the teachings of these conservative Islamic believers. The action caught us completely off guard and that notion was quickly dashed.

"Through DNA testing we've discovered this black man that viciously murdered these people wasn't black at all. He was as white as anyone in this room. The autopsy revealed his skin was pigmented with some sort of a black dye. DNA results confirmed he was Caucasian and the autopsy revealed he had undergone plastic surgery to flatten his nose and had silicone injections to make his lips fuller. His head was shaved.

"Someone has gone to great lengths to disguise this man as an African American specifically intended to carry out this diabolical mission. We've run his DNA and fingerprints through our national data base and haven't been able to identify him. So far, we haven't discovered anything that suggests this man ever existed.

"The Imam leader of the attacked Mosque received, yesterday morning, the same letter your Rabbi here received two days ago. We're still trying to trace this 'Great White Nation' group and have had little success.

"Our fear is that a scenario we have discussed before is becoming a reality. In that scenario we see a group of white supremacists that was formed years ago and have maintained their anonymity. They have raised a generation, maybe two or three generations of sons and daughters who have no public records. I know this sounds impossible in this day and age, but believe me, it is possible. We've discovered families and small groups of religious sects who have done just that.

"If this new generation were raised and educated with hate propaganda and never exposed to the outside world, they'd be the perfect robots to carry out their dictator's orders."

He paused to let what he had just said sink in.

He continued, "What we need, if this scenario is indeed now a reality is a group such as yours to carry out covert and certainly illegal surveillance and operations to eliminate this threat. Even the recently passed terrorist acts don't give our government the necessary authority to completely eliminate this group.

"We will do whatever we can to support and assist you, but without sounding like a recording from 'Mission Impossible' we will deny any knowledge of you if you're caught.

"I'm sure you all have lots of questions and would like to discuss this proposal among yourselves so I suggest we meet here again in the morning."

"Before we consider making some kind of an alliance with your people, we will insist that you divulge who the players on your side are," George Armstrong said and then added, "Mutual trust and an open line of communication is a must."

Rusk nodded and said, "I agree."

"We know you're with the CIA," Chalmers stated, "and we know without your assistance Valerie Kane could never have busted this 'SWI' scandal wide open. Just what is your official position with the CIA and how does your group wield such power?"

"That question, or should I say, those questions I will answer tomorrow, if your group decides to pursue our proposal," Rusk paused and added, "Now, Mary, if you could drive me to my hotel, I'm exhausted. I'm staying at the Mark Hopkins in the City."

Sol stood up and said, "Let's meet at my place in the City tomorrow morning, say ten am. It's more centrally located for everyone."

Once back in the Subaru and heading toward San Francisco, Rusk said, "Mary, tomorrow morning, with your permission, I'm going to suggest that you be allowed to join their team as an active undercover field agent working for the Justice Department. Your assignment will be officially sanctioned. We need an insider who can act as liaison and I'm sure you'd be an asset and accepted by their team."

"Whoa, let me get this straight. You want me to go underground and join their team, with their knowledge, and feed you intelligence?" Dinosa asked incredulously.

"That's about it?" Rusk responded.

Dinosa gripped the wheel tighter and squinted her eyes in thought. They remained silent until they reached the Mark Hopkins' courtyard.

When Rusk pulled the handle to open his door, Dinosa looked at him and said, "Professor, you know you're a conniving old son of a bitch. Valerie's right. You could persuade a Nun out of her habit."

"...So?" he asked feigning embarrassment.

"I'll do it, okay?"

"That's great!" Rusk beamed and leaned over and kissed Dinosa on her forehead.

"How about you and the lovely Ms. Kane join me for dinner tonight at the Top of the Mark?"

"I'll have to check with Valerie. I'll get back to you later," Dinosa said rolling her eyes.

CHAPTER THREE

The choir of the First Gospel Church across the bay in Oakland was in the middle of singing a rousing rendition of 'Get on the Train' when one by one they began coughing.

Sensing something was terribly wrong, some of the congregation started screaming and ran toward the exit at the rear of the church only to find the doors were locked.

Total panic now filled the room and the screams turned into a chorus of uncontrollable coughing. Mothers held their children until they fell to the floor doubled up vomiting in terrible pain. The sounds turned to low moaning and then silence. In less than ten minutes over three hundred men, women and children of the First Gospel Church lay dead on the floor in their house of God.

In the Dining room across the Bay at the Top of the Mark restaurant in San Francisco, Rusk, Kane and Dinosa had just sat down at their table and were ready to order dinner when their cell phones began ringing almost simultaneously.

After they had finished their calls they looked at each other incredulously unable to speak.

Bernard finally broke the silence and said, "I assume we all got similar calls informing us of the tragedy that just occurred in Oakland."

Looking at Kane he asked, "What were your instructions?"

Valerie looked befuddled and responded, "I don't really know. It was from the prosecutor on call from my office and he thought I should know. I suppose I should get to the Federal Building."

"How about you?" he asked Dinosa.

"That was from Ian O'Farrell to tell me about the tragedy and to ask if I was with you and if our meeting tomorrow morning was still on," Dinosa said.

"Tell him yes and you should accompany Valerie and see what you can dig up. I need to get to my room. Can you fetch me about nine in the morning?"

Dinosa appeared lost and then found herself shaking her head and said, "Yes…yes, of course."

—

"I've learned some things about last night's tragedy at the Church in Oakland, but before we get into that I'd like to know if you've come to a decision on the proposal I put to you yesterday?" Rusk said.

George Armstrong looked around the room at his fellow 'Justice Foundation' board members and said, "We've considered your proposal and have unanimously accepted it."

"Excellent," Rusk simply remarked.

Armstrong went on, "Now it's time for you to come clean with us. Who's involved in what you describe as 'some of us in the Capitol' and how far up does it go? Also, what is your agenda?"

"Let me start with our agenda. We are a conscientious group who have all sworn to uphold the U.S. Constitution. We have lost faith with this Administration and where its agenda is taking our Country. We believe, and we're in a good position to know, that the President and the people surrounding him have a dedicated mission to change our Democratic Republic to a Socialist Republic. They look at the trillions of dollars in our national economy that is within their grasp and they look forward to the country going bankrupt. The higher our national debt gets the closer they are to nationalizing our private enterprises and gaining more power and control. They sincerely detest free enterprise and believe they can better manage our national assets.

"We do not trust any of their motivations and we believe they welcome not only the tragedies that have occurred, but any event that will further their agenda and divide the Country. They will use these events as scare tactics aimed at our common constituents and elected officials to pass more laws restricting our individual rights and privacy, similar to what Hitler did to take control of Germany after the 'Treaty of Versailles' and Lenin did after the Russian Revolution.

"As we speak, they are pushing through Congress laws that will erode and in some cases downright eliminate freedoms guaranteed by the first through the fifth Amendments. Through 'Executive Order' they have boldly and without consequence enacted their own laws that circumvent the checks and balances that our forefathers set up as the basics of a free society.

"We have no hidden agenda. We have no aspirations of taking power. We do believe this Administration has done an excellent job of pulling the wool over the eyes of most of America and will not stop until the legislative and judicial systems of this country are mere figure heads.

"I once had a senior Russian Diplomat tell me, 'the problem with you Americans is, you've become such a gullible people. You want to see only the good in people. You want to share your hard earned wealth in the name of charity. Your forefathers immigrated to America with nothing and built a great nation. For some strange reason you now invite foreigners to your country and instead of requiring them to work hard and contribute to your economy and welfare like you and your fathers had to, you give them their existence. The dead beats n your country will soon outnumber the producers and this, my friend, will be your doom.'

"This is a lame duck President. He knows that his time in office is limited and they must act quickly to achieve their transitional form of government. Our group is resolved to prevent that from happening.

"Soon, we plan to reveal the corruption within his administration. We will not stop until he either resigns or is forced out.

"In the meantime, we cannot allow atrocities such as the 'SWI' scandal and now these cowardly hate crimes to go unpunished while our President and his henchmen use them to make speeches and use as a tool to corrupt the system even more."

Rusk paused to allow questions.

"Okay, who are your co-conspirators and how are you so influential?" Goldsmith asked.

"I have been with the CIA on and off for over thirty-five years. During my time in service I have climbed the ladder and have recently been named a Deputy Assistant Director. My boss, William Stuart, has been a lifelong civil servant and after becoming Director under the prior Administration, has managed to, through guile and blackmail, retain his Directorship.

"Together over the years, we have amassed a substantial amount of, shall we say, dirt on government officials and politicians. We have chosen to use this information discretely and in a nonpartisan manner when the offense was so egregious as to jeopardize our national security or form of government. In the process we have found others in high positions that have joined our cause. Among them are the head of the U.S. Marshal Service, several Assistant Deputy Attorney Generals and several Judges on the Supreme Court and a few politicians, including the recently elected U.S. Representative from the State of Colorado, John Garcia. We also have a mole inside the Whitehouse who keeps us apprised of their tactics.

"Gentlemen, our resources are nearly infinite, which is how we've been able to track your missions and movements."

"Well, so much for our security, tell us what you've learned about the tragedy in Oakland and the other atrocities committed by this so called 'Great White Nation'," Ian said.

"Our sources, Mary Dinosa here being one of them, tell us the police found a canister linked to an intake vent of the air conditioning system in the men's room on the first floor of the Church. The canister contained a mixture of an extremely deadly form of serine gas and a yet to be determined element. The canister was equipped with an electronic valve remotely controlled. Those poor souls had a very painful death, but it was over quickly.

"The exit doors had been bolted down from the outside. Several witnesses saw two men dressed in black fatigues running down the Church's entrance steps at about 7:30 pm, or shortly before the canister's valve was opened, and jump in a black or dark colored van and speed away.

"It's been confirmed the Pastor of the Church had received, earlier yesterday, a duplicate of the letter sent to the leader of the San Francisco Synagogue and the New York Mosque. It was found, opened on his desk.

"The letter and envelope have been sent to the FBI lab in Washington, D.C., as have the others, for processing. The only common substance found on the first two letters was some pollen residue from the Ponderosa Pine tree subspecies known as the Northern Plateau Ponderosa. That particular subspecies grows predominantly in the northwest and south western Canada.

"That means our hate group's headquarters are most likely located somewhere in south eastern British Columbia, north eastern Washington, northern Idaho or western Montana."

"That certainly narrows down our search zone," Ian said sarcastically and then went on, "What do you want us to do?"

"There's not a lot you can do right now. You and your team can study their tactics which may prove helpful when we launch field maneuvers and you might pick up on something that could tell us where and how they got their training.

"I'd like to borrow Doctor Tanaka for a while. We could team him with a friend of mine who's a Professor working in the Genetics Research facility at Stanford University.

He has the genetic markers from the New York perpetrator's DNA results and thinks he may be able to link them to a family tree, but the numbers are mind boggling. It's way above my head, but he knows of Doctor Tanaka and says that with his computer expertise it could cut down the time frame tremendously.

"Also, I suggest that Ms. Dinosa join your field operations' team. Officially she'll be working undercover as an agent of the Justice Department. Here's the caveat; I know she's worked with you before and she holds our mutual respect. There may be, and probably will be, times that communication between myself and your group could compromise our mission. Mary can act as our liaison and her undercover status would distance ourselves from one another and accommodate deniability if anything should go south."

The group looked at one another and nodded in agreement.

Sean smiled and said, "Once again Ms. Dinosa, welcome aboard."

CHAPTER FOUR

JULY 8, 1968—HAYFORK, ARKANSAS:

The inner council of the district's chapter of the Klu Klux Klan sat at an oval table in the town's community center. Present were eight men donned in different colored robes designating their rank within the clan.

The man dressed in the gold robe at the head of the table began, "We all know the seriousness of this meeting. Gentlemen we are losing our Holy War against the northern Yankees who are sweep'n in to destroy our way of life, our religion and our segregate'n ways. Just last week the Sheriff of our neighboring Carter County and two of his deputies were arrested by the FBI for ridding our community of those college kid vermin who invaded our land. Those kids were sent here to overlook our election by their cowardly mothers and fathers and them and their likes needed to be taught a lesson.

"Our children's mothers and fathers are not cowards. We will, of course, stand by our convictions and fight till the last man stands, but our numbers are decreas'n. These liberal Jezebels have infiltrated our schools and our churches and have perverted the minds of our Negroes. Our mission is to ensure that some of our numbers survive this war.

"Brother Frank, are you ready to lead our children to the Promised Land!"

Frank Johnson, sitting to the right of the man in the gold colored robe, rose and said solemnly, "Yes, I am."

"Bring in the four," the gold robe ordered.

A man guarding the door to the room opened it and motioned for the four young men donned in white robes to enter. They stood next to the table.

The gold robe smiled and said, "You are the chosen few. You are the soldiers and with your wives you will follow Frank and venture forth into the land of Canaan. You have bravely volunteered for this mission and we will miss you, but know you are our last line of defense. You will forever be in our prayers and we will support you in your times of need, but contact with your family here will cease now and until you are rejoined in Heaven. If we are to prevail, you must prevail. You are the roots of the new 'GREAT WHITE NATION'."

...And so began the birth of the neo-nation. The five couples traveled north and settled on a two thousand acre parcel of land in the northern region of the Idaho panhandle where the Cascade Mountains meet the Great Rocky Mountains. Frank Johnson had purchased the piece of land with money he had withdrawn from a trust fund set up by his family.

The property was located in a valley surrounded on three sides with mountains and Gold Miners Creek bordered the southern open side. The only access was an old slightly improved logging road that wound down the valley and met the thoroughfare three miles away.

The Johnson family had made a fortune in the coal mining business in Arkansas and Tennessee and Frank's family continued to covertly deposit money in his trust fund with the knowledge that it was being used to build the 'Great White Nation' which would be the savior of them all.

The new pioneers proved to be an industrious lot and set about creating a self-sustained community where they could raise their families without outside interference. They home birthed and educated their babies. The only birth records were kept in a secret family log to insure no future inbreeding.

Wind generators were erected to provide their scant electrical requirements and gardens were cultivated to provide them with vegetables. Meat and fish were plentiful in their wilderness surroundings and so was the hate they taught and spewed to their children along with their biblical interpretations and faith.

A ten foot high cyclone fence topped with bob wire and well posted with 'No Trespassing' signs surrounded their compound. They were completely isolated from the outside world with the exception of a Johnson family courier who lived in nearby Bonners Ferry and who owned a gun and outdoorsmen store in the rural town.

All of the men in the compound were ex-military men highly trained in assault, guerilla and insurgency tactics and were Viet Nam veterans. They had brought their training and military manuals with them and raised their sons from birth as if they were in a military academy.

Through the years their numbers increased and after three generations their population totaled over one hundred, twenty-two of whom were now young men well trained and indoctrinated with hate. Recently, Frank Johnson announced that the war must begin.

Over the years they had stockpiled a large cache of weapons and explosives and stashed them in caves dug into the mountain side. One large cavern had been constructed as a gunnery range and training area. Here they could conduct their training out of sight of prying eyes.

Government agencies like the Census Bureau, the IRS and Child Protective Services were beginning to intrude on their way of life. Legal and counter legal action and court injunctions had in the past prevailed in their favor, but Frank Johnson could see the writing on the wall.

He drew his followers together and announced, "As the Prophet Isaiah predicted, '…And the Kingdom of the North and the Kingdom of the South shall wage a great war. And because the Kingdom of the North is God's chosen people they shall prevail'. I say to you now, that day has arrived and all the training and planning we have prepared for will now pay dividends. We declare WAR on the infidels and sinners of the south!"

—

CHAPTER FIVE

Doctors Daniel Tanaka and Theodore Bernstein made an interesting and diverse pair. Dr. Tanaka was a tall gangly Japanese American man from Hilo, Hawaii, who is a Professor of Computer Sciences and Doctor Bernstein is a short and stout Jewish American man from the Eastside of Manhattan, New York, who is a Professor of Genetics at Stanford University. The only things they have in common is an intense, almost a compulsive curiosity in their chosen fields and both are respected as being the best in their respective fields.

Although they had just recently met, they were well aware of who the other one was by reputation and instantly formed a bond.

Doctor Tanaka, who preferred to go by the name 'Grub', a handle he was given as a kid because of his unkempt appearance that stayed with him as he grew older, after his illustrious academic career had taken a position with a high tech computer company before going free-lance and starting a consulting firm with his new bride, Belinda 'Snoopy' Grant.

The two had met several years ago after Grub was recruited to work with the 'Justice Foundation' in their pursuit of the 'North Beach Killer' and was teamed with Snoopy who was an IT Tech with the SFPD and at the time a member of the police task force investigating the serial murderer.

The grandparents of Doctor Bernstein emigrated from Norway in nineteen-forty ahead of the Nazi takeover and the slaughter of many of their relatives. They settled in New York City and opened a kosher deli shop. Theodore's parents later took over running the deli until their untimely deaths at the hands of a crazed drug addicted man who shot them both while robbing the store.

Theodore, who preferred to be called Teddy, was an eight year old only child at the time and with no living relatives in the United States, he was promptly adopted by his parent's closest friends and neighbors who worshipped together in the same Synagogue, Bernard and Sarah Rusk. The Rusk's raised him as their own with the rest of their family.

Teddy proved to be a special 'genius' child, graduating from high school at twelve and becoming the youngest ever Professor in his field receiving his Doctorate in genetic science at eighteen. Now, at thirty years old, he was the head of the Medical Genetics Research Department at the Stanford University Medical Center in Palo Alto, California. He preferred research and delegated his administrative duties to capable others.

The odd pair along with Snoopy and Teddy's most able research assistant, Catharina Domingo, was now gathered around a table in the corner of a large room in the basement of George Armstrong's mansion in Los Gatos, California.

The room had been transformed into a laboratory that most universities would be proud to have. Grub and Snoopy had installed an isolated and standalone computer network that communicated within the walls of the lab only. Any outside data was gathered and downloaded independently from their network and then that input was disconnected before connected and uploaded to the system's network. The standalone system was hard wired and could not facilitate a wireless connection.

Grub simply explained it to George Armstrong by saying, "It assures us that no one from the outside can hack our system."

"So far, we have isolated strands of the DNA from the unknown New York attacker provided by Bernie. This sample is but a starting point. Much to my displeasure," he continued, glancing at Catherina, "our work won't be an exact science."

Teddy continued, "Besides the DNA, Bernie has provided us with blood, urine, feces, flesh, lung, liver and bone marrow samples. The results of our tests may or may not help us in determining, among other things, where this gentleman is from.

"Thanks to you two," he said, looking at Grub and Snoopy, "we are equipped with the state of the art computer system. From here it will be a process of elimination."

"We've been able to hack every available DNA data base in the country with Bernie's help, and downloaded the profiles of over thirty million samples from military, criminal and every alphabet agency in existence.

"I've developed a complicated logarithm program that can cross compare marker similarities. The more markers we get the more sample DNA profiles we can eliminate. Teddy, that's your job," Grub said.

"Well then, let's get to work," Teddy sighed.

—

"The results of the ATF inspection of the weapon used in New York say it was a modified version of the AR16. Most of the alterations they've never seen before which leaves them to believe they were made by an excellent gun smith with access to some fairly sophisticated tools and machinery.

"The breech had been modified to accept a shorter cartridge that would accept the home made rounds and a one hundred capacity spiral clip. The standard stock had been replaced with a fold up style and the barrel had been shortened and fire suppressor removed to accommodate easy concealment.

"This weapon was designed for one purpose. Without a front site that purpose was to provide close in fire protection to kill as many random targets as possible in the shortest amount of time. It's similar to the Israeli Uzi, but with a lot more deadly force," Ian Armstrong addressed his fellow team members in the basement gym of his father's manor.

He continued, "The ammunition would be fairly easy to make. You'd just have to take a standard AR16 shell and cut down the casing and refill it with less powder and reattach any same diameter bullet. In this case the bullets were molded lead with a hollow point meant to separate on impact and cause maximum damage.

"The round spiral clip is another story. The workmanship tells us it was definitely home made, but it would still require a metal bender and arch welder. It was a disposable clip that can be used only once. The feeder spring repressor is manually removed upon loading and would make it practically impossible to reload in the field.

"These assholes know what they're doing. It's hard to say what kind of training they've undergone, but there is some military influence involved. All of their missions so far have been well planned, rehearsed and carried out. When we meet up with these pricks we'll be facing a formidable enemy."

—

"Mary, I'm afraid I've put you in a very dangerous position," Bernard Rusk said gravely.

He was sitting in a corner booth inside 'Lefty's Tavern' in San Francisco's Tenderloin District with Mary Dinosa and Chuck Chalmers.

"Geez Bernie, why do I get the feeling you're about to wake up and slip out the back door and not even leave your number?" Dinosa queried sarcastically.

"We have reason to believe," Rusk said seriously, ignoring her snide remark, "our group has been penetrated. To what degree and how it might affect us we haven't determined. Secrets in the Capitol are hard to keep.

"People in the Administration, for example, have considered me their enemy for years, but they also know the secrets I hold which to this point have kept them at bay. It's actually been to our advantage. Nervous people make mistakes.

"The President's Security Council is a group of individuals appointed by and very close and loyal to the President. They yield a tremendous amount of power and influence. Their ability to raise money to keep the President in power is mind blowing. Guess where the majority of the billions of dollars wasted on the 'bail out' and busted 'green energy' policies went? To the same people who contributed millions to the President's reelection campaign and his party. But I'm getting off track."

He paused to take a sip of beer and continued, "The people sitting on the Security Council are becoming paranoid. They have launched an all-out effort to determine how deep and extensive our group is and the threat we present.

"We don't believe they've discovered who you are Mary, but they're very suspicious of you and," he said looking at Chalmers, "we're sure they haven't uncovered any knowledge of the 'Justice Foundation'. We don't think your mission had been compromised.

"That said, we have to proceed with even more caution. Mary, we have assigned a very capable team to act as a TOT, or tail on the tail. It's best you do not know their identities. Their assignment will be to follow you to determine if you're being followed and to protect you. Maintain your current security protocol, but don't give away that you think that you may be a target. Our means of communication will remain the same, but you're communication with the Foundation will change.

"Your romantic connection with Ian Armstrong will be our means to interchange information. You two have already established a known relationship and your meetings won't raise suspicions. Henceforth, your only communication with the Foundation will be with Ian."

Turning again towards Chalmers, he said, "Your group has done a great job of keeping your anonymity. When the dust has settled, we'll have to study your methods."

"Let me get this straight. This," Dinosa said shaking her head, "TOT who I don't know who they are, will be following me to catch someone following me and I'm supposed to ignore all of them and go about my daily business and meet with my lover to communicate covert information?"

"I couldn't have put it better," Rusk said with a smile.

—

Mary Dinosa felt like a goldfish in a bowl on public display. She had always prided herself of being in control of her life and her situation, but the last two days since Rusk had informed her that her every step was being observed and probably documented, she felt anxious and angry.

She had to force herself not to glance over her shoulder as she opened the door and entered 'Lefty's Tavern'. She spotted Ian sitting at what had become their table in the corner of the bar.

She took a chair at the table and sitting down, said with a sigh, "Have you ever had that dream where you're the only naked person in the middle of a crowded room?"

"No, but I'd like to be one of the people in that room," Ian replied with a chuckle.

"Ha fucking ha," Dinosa said with a sneer.

Ian's expression turned serious and he said, "Don't look now, but the guy who just came in must be the one following you and I know him."

"Jesus, who the hell is he?" Dinosa said fighting even harder the urge to look around.

"His name is Al Long. He was an Army Ranger, Special Forces Captain. We did a combined special op to liberate a family being held by a gang of pirates in a Somalia camp a few years back," Ian said and continued, "I heard he retired and took a position with a private defense contracting firm. He's one bad son of a bitch."

Al Long took a seat at the bar and without surveying the room ordered a drink. Ian got up immediately and took the chair with his back towards the bar. Dinosa pulled out a cell phone and dialed Rusk's number.

While she was on the phone she noticed Long catch her eye as he was being joined by another man.

After a short phone conversation, Dinosa disconnected and feigning a loud laugh and through a wide smile she lowered he voice and said, "Bernie says you should confront him as a long lost combat buddy and how surprised you are to meet him here of all places."

"What?" Ian exclaimed.

"Bernie thinks it can't hurt anything and by confronting him, he and his buddy will be compromised and have to be replaced. Who knows how these spooks think? Just do it."

After a moment of pondering, Ian pushed his chair back and stood up.

"I'm going to the powder room, I'll be back," he said in his best 'Arnold' impersonation.

As he turned around he noticed both men glance away. When he approached the two men he passed them and then stopped and backed up a step. Long looked up at him.

Ian stuck out his hand and said loudly, "Al, Al Long, you old dog faced son of a bitch!"

Long pulled back and looked at Ian. He doesn't recognize me, Ian realized.

"I'm Ian Armstrong, U.S. Navy retired. We met off the coast of Somalia about five years ago in a joint op."

With a look of recognition, Long said, "Oh yeah, shit! Pull up a stool."

Turning back to his friend he said, "Peter McCoy, meet Ian Armstrong. He's the swabbie I was telling you about. We extracted some people held in a Somalia camp it seems like a century ago."

"Nice to meet you," Ian said nodding at Long's companion and continued, "Sorry I can't join you. I'm with my girlfriend. Are you living in the area?"

"No, I'm retired from the army and just looking for a job. My buddy, Peter, and I are just tourists visiting your great city." Long lied.

"Well, it was great seeing you. I've got to drain the dragon and get back to my date. Take care of yourself," Ian said shaking Long's hand again.

When Ian came out of the men's room Al Long and his friend were gone.

—

CHAPTER SIX

The two young men were ushered into what they called the 'Command Chamber'. It was a grotto which had been blasted and dug out into the granite mountain side at the end of a long tunnel from the cave called the 'Community Center'.

The entire compound consisted of inter connecting tunnels and self-contained living quarter grottoes that expanded over the years as the 'Great White Nation' grew. Only one large two story home, occupied by the original five couples, stood outside of the cave community along with a large barn.

The two young men stood at attention next to an oval table where five men dressed in robes sat.

Frank Johnson, who had changed his name to Joshua and was showing his seventy years of life on earth sat at the head of the table and addressed his two young soldiers, "Because of your intelligence and dedication to the 'Great White Nation', you have been chosen to be the two Shittim spies and venture forth into Jericho to retrieve the harlot, Rahab, and bring her to us."

Joshua motioned for the two young men to come closer and opened a file sitting in front of him.

"This is information provided to us by our spy entrenched in Washington, D.C.," he started and continued, "He believes our enemies are getting closer to identifying us and our location. He has identified the harlot Rahab as one of the people looking for us. Your mission is to abduct her and bring her to us. This folder contains her picture, address, where she works and her given name, Mary Dinosa."

—

"We've decided to relocate the operation's team," Sean Armstrong said.

He went on, "We are convinced that these yahoos are located somewhere in the northwest and we hope to pinpoint their location soon and believe you should be more centrally located. When the time comes we will have to move fast."

The team and the Foundation members were gathered in the basement gymnasium of the O'Farrell manor.

"We've leased an abandoned hunting lodge on the banks of Lake Coeur d'Alene, Idaho, not far from the town by the same name. Be prepared to leave in a couple of hours," Solomon Goldsmith added.

"Since the people tailing Mary Dinosa have been compromised and our TOT tells us they haven't been replaced yet, we're bringing her here tonight for her protection and for the duration of the operation," Ian said.

Chalmers asked, "What progress have Grub and Teddy made?"

"Don't ask me how they've done it, but they've pared the genetic markers from the unknown donor down to less than one hundred families. Grub has developed criteria from family histories that should further eliminate origins. Sounds like it won't take much longer," George Armstrong said.

"Okay," Ian said standing up, "Let's pack our shit."

—

"I'd like to welcome everyone. This may be the last chance we'll have to meet as a group for a while, so let's get down to business," Bernard Rusk said to begin the meeting.

Sitting around the table inside a conference room at CIA headquarters in Langley, Virginia was a group of Washington insiders that as individuals did not yield a lot of power, but together held the ability to topple the present Administration because of their collected positions, information and intelligence. Among their numbers present was an Assistant Deputy Attorney General, a member of the President's Security Council, a District DEA Superintendent, a sitting member of the U.S. Commerce Department, the board president of a major television network, and several members of the U.S. Congress including John Garcia, recently elected Representative from Colorado who ran on a drug law reformation platform and was a former DEA Agent and member of the 'Justice Foundation'.

Rusk went on, "George Armstrong sends his regrets that he could not be with us, but I think we all can appreciate that he's legitimately busy with his group in California and their efforts to take down this 'Great White Nation'.

"Speaking of that situation, I'd like to report that we are getting very close to identifying them. Doctors Tanaka and Bernstein have narrowed the search of the unknown subject's DNA to an Arkansas family with ties to the KKK. They're investigating that family's history and with any luck they should produce a report any day now."

He answered several questions regarding that family's name and the current status of the 'Justice Foundation's' progress. He explained the team had been relocated to northern Idaho and the reasons for doing that and they had decided to bring Mary Dinosa into the safe house.

He could and would order a Defense Department Satellite to be positioned in a geosynchronous orbit when the 'Great White Nation's' location was discovered that would provide the team with 24/7 surveillance, saying, "That assumes the climate cooperates and there's no cloud cover."

John Garcia reported that his 'Narcotics Reform Act' had passed the House with little opposition and was now before the Senate.

"The President and his team have distanced themselves from the situation and the debate. After the sacrificial lambs they served up after the political payoff scandal they have no stomach to interfere with us.

"I must say, the actions of the 'Justice Foundation' and the Valerie Kent's prosecutions have put a serious dent in the Administration's war fund. The drug cartels are in complete disarray and on the run. The fall out has resulted in a drastic increase in the price of street drugs in this country and a dramatic increase in crime, but as soon as the new laws take effect we will see these numbers decrease substantially," Garcia concluded.

The next hour was taken up with discussions about the information and intelligence the group had gathered and strategies on when and how it would be divulged.

Rusk concluded the meeting by saying, "I believe we are all agreed that the "Jesus Come to Meeting" is fast approaching. Doctor Tanaka and his wife Belinda have assembled all of our information and a list of recipients to receive it upon our go ahead.

"At this point in time, regardless of what may become of us, you may rest assured the truth will come out."

—

"Mom, do you think Pop will be back by Christmas?" Jennifer asked, sitting between her two friends Matthew and Shannon in the back seat of the SUV.

In the front seat sat their mothers, Sheila Lamont driving and Colleen Chalmers in the passenger seat. They were traveling south on Highway Five still a couple of hours from the O'Farrell estate.

"I hope so," Colleen sighed.

"You know," Jennifer went on, "I've always used his trips as an excuse to get something. This time all I want is for him to come home safely and kill all of those terrorist sons of bitches!"

"Jennifer Lynn, you watch your mouth!" Colleen screeched, trying to suppress a smile.

"You know that is impossible, I mean 'watching my mouth'," Jennifer retorted.

The group burst into nervous laughter.

—

As the foundation operations team boarded their private Cessna Citation jet at San Francisco International Airport that would take them to the airport in Coeur d'Alene, Idaho, Chad Carbahol sat in his car parked across the street watching Mary Dinosa pull up to the gate guarding the entrance to her apartment garage off Third Street in San Francisco. A gentle rain was falling on his windshield partially obstructing his view.

He watched as she swiped a card through a scanner and the gate swung open. She pulled into the garage, parked at her assigned space and walked to the freight elevator that would take her to her converted loft apartment in the old remodeled warehouse.

She disappeared into the elevator. She emerged into her open studio apartment she shared with her black and white cat named Tuxedo. Her suspicions were aroused when Tuxedo wasn't there to greet her with his usual complaint while he rubbed against her leg.

Without switching on the light, she reached under her windbreaker and produced her duty weapon. Proceeding cautiously into the room she said, "Tux, where are you little guy?"
She heard a metallic plink and felt a sting in her buttocks.

"Ah sit," she said, turning around to see from where and by whom the dart had originated.

Her vision blurred and she felt dizzy. Before collapsing to the floor, her last thought was, "How could I be so fucking stupid?"

A man emerged from the darkness of a corner and another from a closet on the opposite side of the room.

Carbahol sat waiting in his car. His assignment was to tail and observe anyone that might be tailing Mary Dinosa and to protect her. He was the TOT.

Chad had served eight years in the U.S. Army Special Services and for the two years before he got out was attached to the CIA and participated in black ops in Iraq and Afghanistan. That's when his handler, Bernard Rusk convinced him to get out of the Army and join his team.

He now received his orders directly from George Armstrong and for the last two and a half years his assignments had been to observe and report activities of the 'Justice Foundation's' field and tactical team.

It had been a curious and exciting journey, taking him from San Francisco to the swamps of Florida, to a Caribbean island, to Mexico several times and other various parts of the world.

He was a dedicated soldier, but often wondered what effect he had on the accomplishments of Ian Armstrong and his team. He certainly admired them as exemplary peers.

He knew Mary Dinosa would be joining the rest of the group at the O'Farrell estate and she was just picking up some things from home before going there. He would give her ten minutes before getting anxious.

After eleven minutes he got out of his car and crossed the street to the building's main entrance. He rang her apartment and after getting no response he jimmied the lock, careful not to show his face to the camera that observed the entrance. The door opened to a small foyer with a hall leading off on one side and a flight of stairs to the other.

He climbed the stairs to the third floor landing where one door stood at the end of a short hallway. He jimmied the door and stepped in removing a 9 mm handgun from beneath his coat. He glanced around the room in the dark and then switching on the light said, "Mary, it's a friend."

Searching the room he found no evidence of Dinosa, but did find the cat hiding under the bed. He ran to a double glass door and saw it led to a lanai with an attached fire escape that ascended to an alley behind the building.

He reached in his pocket and pulled out a cell phone. After dialing he said, "George, its Chad. I'm in her apartment and she's disappeared."

After he explained the details of the evenings events, Armstrong replied, "Ah shit, it must be the 'GWN'. Stay there and I'll meet you in half an hour, I think it's about time you come out of the shadows."

Chad spent his time waiting trying to coax Tuxedo from beneath the bed.

—

Sean O'Farrell opened his front door and was facing George Armstrong and another rather large man holding a pet carrier. George introduced him as Chad Carbahol.

"So this is the TOT?" Sean said with a smile.

Sean escorted the two men to the den and along the way George said, "I apologize for not letting the group know about my unofficial connection with the CIA and my longtime friendship with Bernard Rusk, but I believed at the time that anonymity was more important. You probably figured it out anyway."

"Yes we, or should I say Mary Dinosa, did. She put two and two together shortly after Bernard became involved with the sting operation. We knew, in time, you would come clean."

Sol Goldsmith was waiting for them in the den. Upon being introduced he noticed Chad's left hand was wrapped with gauze.

He commented, "What happened to your hand?"

"It seems Mary's furry friend is as ferocious as his owner. It's a small scratch," Chad replied.

Ian said, "Well, we've alerted Ian and the team that Mary's been abducted. You think it was the GWN?"

"It almost has to be. The only intel we've received from our man in the Capitol was orders to tail her, not kidnap her.," George said.

"That certainly puts us in a position to waste no time," Goldsmith said gravely.

"Now that I've been outed, I'd like to be a member of your team," Chad said and continued, "Even though I haven't met Ms. Dinosa face to face, I've come to know her and other team members quite well over the past several years. I feel partially responsible for her disappearance and it would be an honor if I could join the effort in retrieving her."

PART II

THE BATTLES

"The war is not won at the peace tables, but by the battles on the beaches and in the fox holes." Attributed to General George Patton

CHAPTER SEVEN

Chalmers could feel the foul mood of his fellow team members as they unloaded their gear from the van and trudged across the snowy gravel driveway to the lodge's front door. He noticed Ian O'Farrell was particularly tight lipped and appeared ready to explode.

They were greeted at the door by an older couple who introduced themselves as Jim and Judy Cox.

"We've been hired on as caretakers of this here establishment and been try'n to straighten up a bit before your arrival. Judy here, was the cook and I was the chief hunt'n guide back when this was a bustl'n outfitters business.

"Sol Goldsmith used to bring his group up every year to go hunt'n. He's the one who called and hired us on. We're stay'n in the caretaker's cabin just over yonder on the lake. If you need anything, just holler."

With that, he and his wife departed with a wave.

The group found themselves standing inside a large open room. The wall on the left was mostly grouted rock with a fireplace and mantel in the center. A warm fire was burning in the fireplace and firewood was stacked beside it. A kitchen sat on the opposite side with an eight man dinner table in between and a sitting area with a couch and several easy chairs off to one side. A stairway located next to the front door led to a loft area upstairs that accommodated four bunk beds and an enclosed bathroom.

The four men filed up the stairs and each claimed a lower bunk and started unpacking and stowing their gear.

Chalmers cell phone rang and he answered, "Chalmers here."

"Yeah Chuck, its Sean, I take it your settled in the lodge by now. How is everybody?"

"We're a little crabby and tired. Other than that we're doing just hunky dory. Any word on Mary?"

Sean rolled his eyes, but said in a calm voice, "We're almost certain that Mary was taken by the GWN and we think they'll keep her alive. If they wanted her dead our TOT would have found here in her apartment."

"TOT, we know who the TOT is!?" Chalmers demanded.

"Yes, and I'll get into that later. We think Dinosa is heading to your part of the world and we're getting real close to determining her destination. You guys need to just sit tight."

"Yeah, well you can tell that to your son."

Upon hearing that, Ian extended his hand and said, "May I talk with him?"

"Dad, what's up?" Ian asked.

His father reiterated what he'd just said to Chalmers and added the identity and the story surrounding the TOT. He concluded by saying, "Son, he's a comrade in arms and he'll be joining your group. His name is Chad Carbahol and he's driving up and should be their sometime tomorrow. We'll leave it up to you on how you want to use him."

Ian turned toward the group and said, "Let's go down stairs and try to get comfortable and I'll brief you."

—

"Hey, Jed, wake up. It's your turn to drive."

The words seemed to echo from a distance. At first Dinosa thought it was her father's voice waking her up to go to school. That can't be right, she thought. She hasn't been in school for years and why can't I open my mouth and why is it so dark?

She suddenly remembered the recent events. The sting in her butt and drawing her weapon and seeing the man emerge from her closet and then nothing. How long had she been out? Where was she? Her mouth was now taped and her arms tied behind her and ankles tied together. A hood of some kind covered her head.

She realized she was in a moving vehicle. She started to panic and wriggled to free herself and then stopped. Better if her captors thought she was still out. She realized the benefit of surprise was probably her only ally.

She heard and felt the road surface change to gravel and the vehicle slow down and roll to a stop.

Another voice sleepily said, "Where are we?"

The reply came, "We just passed through Jordan Valley, Oregon. Still have another ten hours before we're home. Check on our passenger and see how she's doing."

Jed moved between the seats and crawled to the rear of the van and knelt beside Dinosa. He lifted the hood up and Dinosa remained still. He slapped her face hard and she still didn't respond.

"She's still out," he said and then chuckled, "but she peed her pants."

Dinosa for the first time felt the cold dampness between her legs. Ah shit, she thought, you mother fuckers are gonna pay for this.

—

CHAPTER EIGHT

"Mr. President, for the record I've ensured this is officially recorded as our routine daily briefing. I'm here to discuss your pending gun legislature and upcoming speech to the U.N."

"For Christ sake Paulie, drop the formalities. It's just the two of us here."

Paulo Santiago had met the President twenty some years ago when they both attended Detroit City College and became fast friends on the school's debating team. They shared political beliefs and ambitions. He saw the potential in his new friend's uncanny charisma and power of persuasion and connections.

He hitched his wagon to his new found friend's train and followed him to Harvard University and back to Detroit where they worked as political organizers for the party. He was with him when he was elected a City Alderman, then a first term U.S. Senator and was named his Chief of Staff when his friend was elected the President of the United States.

"I'm sorry Barry, but I didn't want you to shoot the messenger," Paulo said with a nervous smile.

"I'm sure we've gotten through worse situations. What's up?"

The President's coolness under fire was the attribute Paulo most admired about his friend. He exuded confidence and it was catching. The hotter it got, the cooler he got.

"We have a spy in our midst. I would have never believed Steve Caldwell would have turned on us. I mean, he goes back to Detroit with us for Christ sake. He swore his allegiance to us," Paulo moaned.

The President stroked his chin and only a slight flare of his nostrils hinted at the rage erupting inside him. He glanced up at the ceiling of the Oval Office and then turned his chair and stared out the window.

After a long pause, he turned his chair back around facing Paulo and calmly asked, "To whom and what has he divulged?"

"He was discovered by pure accident. He was observed by a member of my staff passing an envelope to a woman at the Lincoln Memorial yesterday. My staff member recognized the woman as someone who works for Bernard Rusk. We have to assume he's passed on everything he knows.

"That would include our strategy to use the latest hate group tragedies to build public outrage and support for your recommended legislation and our covert efforts to stymie the FBI and Homeland Security investigations," Paulo replied, trying to emulate the President's calm demure.

"What's my exposure?" the President asked.

"I believe we can claim yours and my credible deniability, but it will require the sacrifice of some of our people," Paulo said gravely.

"I'll need a list of those people, and Paulie, for the better good, Steve Caldwell will have to pay the supreme sacrifice," the President said, looking Paulo in the eyes.

"Understood, Mr. President, that situation is being addressed," Paulo said, standing to leave.

—

The following morning under the headline *JUNIOR WHITEHOUSE STAFF MEMBER COMMITS SUICIDE,* the Washington Sentinel reported on page six;

Steven Caldwall (sic), a junior member of the presidential staff, was found shot to death in his Georgetown apartment late last night. Police authorities announced the coroner's office has determined a single self-inflicted gunshot was the cause of death.

A statement released from the White House stated, "The President is deeply grieved by hearing this news and extends his condolences to the family, friends and loved ones of Steve."

An anonymous source close to the president was quoted as saying, "I know Steve had been recently diagnosed with an inoperable cancerous brain tumor. We believe, after hearing the treatment he faced and the survival possibilities, he chose what he thought was the honorable way out. He will be greatly missed by those of us who knew and worked with him."

Mr. Caldwell, a decorated Army Staff Sergeant during the Gulf War, joined the President's team as a staff member going back to the President's early political career in Detroit, Michigan.

—

"Damn, Bernie, they're getting desperate! Do you believe any of the media reporting?" George Armstrong said.

"You mean what little reporting by the media, and no I don't believe a word of it," Rusk replied and continued, "Steve was a friend and a loyal American and before this is over he will be bigger news than a four paragraph story buried in the newspaper.

"Their desperation is the reason I chanced the trip out here," he said, sitting in an easy chair in Armstrong's den. "The President and Paulo Santiago believe they're isolated and untouchable. The arrogant, narcissistic bastards think they're above accountability and are willing to go to any lengths to keep it that way. As you know, we're on the verge of exposing them and changing that.

"I was going to ask you to suspend or at least delay your operation against the GWN until after our mission is completed, but since the abduction of Mary Dinosa, I know that option is out of the equation.

"Where are we in locating the GWN?"

"Grub and Teddy have narrowed the DNA down to a specific family. Their research and investigation has come up with, according to Grub's calculation, a possibility factor of eighty-eight point umpteen decimals that he is a descendant of a specific Johnson family from Hayfork, Arkansas. They discovered a member of that family named Frank Kilgore Johnson, along with three or more other local families, dropped off the grid in the late sixties. As far as anybody knows, they have disappeared and the trail goes dead.

"However, they have tracked another Johnson family member, a cousin of Frank Johnson. About the same time as his cousin disappeared he relocated with his family to Bonners Ferry, Idaho, and opened a gun and sport store. We believe he may be the GWI liaison with the outside world.

"These people are not Arkansas hillbillies. They hail from big coal money and have almost unlimited funds. Grub thinks he's close to finding out how they are funneling funds to the GWN."

"What can we do?" Rusk asked.

"After briefing the team we asked them the same question. We've already complied with their munitions requests and a national APB has been issued on the disappearance of Mary Dinosa.

"I told them that we'd position a surveillance satellite over Bonners Ferry for fast positioning once we've pin pointed the

GWN location. Unfortunately, this time of the year means the weather will be mostly cloudy there, so they know they'll be able to use the satellite as a tool, but they can't rely on it."

"Now that we no longer have Steve in their circle, we'll have no intelligence to warn us if the foundation's team is discovered. We need a contingency plan, should that happen. Have you given that any thought?" Armstrong asked.

"Actually we have and we do. It may come late and it may be inadequate, but Chad has a good friend who is the District Supervising Agent with the FBI in that area. Without disclosing any of the mission, he's been assured he'll be informed by his friend if any unusual orders come down the chain of command," Rusk replied and added, "George, I'm not sure how religious you are but a prayer at this time wouldn't hurt."

"Amen and God speed," Armstrong whispered sincerely.

—

"Bonners Ferry…? Son of a bitch, I know the Chief of Police there," Chalmers exclaimed upon hearing the team's destination. "We used to be partners in the SFPD. His name is Dwight Bradley MacArthur."

"You gotta be shit'n me. Who the hell would put that tag on their kid and why would he take a job as Police Chief in a Podunk town?" Grant said with a chuckle.

"Speculation around the SFPD surrounding how he got his name was his father was a WWII vet and he probably thought he was honoring somebody. Maybe he just had a helluva weird sense of humor. Mack had three or four ex-wives he was supporting with alimony payments and approaching mandatory retirement with the department he was probably forced to take a job. Let that be a lesson to the rest of you young fellows. Don't let your dicks get in the way of your retirement," Chalmers advised to the laughter of the group.

Chad Carbahol knocked on and then entered the front door of the lodge. He introduced himself and was quickly pulled aside by Ian.

"How the hell did you let Mary get captured?" Ian whispered through clenched teeth.

Through squinted eyes, Carbahol replied, "First of all, I didn't 'let Mary get captured', and secondly it doesn't matter how she got captured, it's how do we get her back."

Ian eased his grip on Chad's arm and then let it go when Carbahol said, "Commander, I know when I'm being played. Did I pass, sir?"

With a smile now, Ian said, "Yes you did Captain, and drop the sir shit. I actually work for a living these days. By the way, since I found out your identity I had a friend do a little digging. We actually came close to meeting, once in Somalia and once in Afghanistan."

"I know," Chad replied with a wink.

"Okay everybody, let's load up. Jesse, you and Grant and our new found member here, Carbahol, will be traveling in the mobile surveillance van and Ian and I will be following in the SUV. We'll meet up at the Flying J truck stop on the outskirts of Bonners Ferry just south of town off Interstate Ninety-Five," Chalmers said, picking up a duffle bag and heading toward the front door.

—

CHAPTER NINE

President Barrymore Jasper Benjamin was born in Detroit, Michigan, in 1970. He was the result of a short lived affair between his mother, Janine Benjamin, and the son of an executive of one of the big three Detroit automobile manufacturers for whom his mother worked for as a resident domestic.

Upon hearing of her pregnancy, his father's family promptly dismissed his mother, and with the understanding that she would never divulge her son's birth right, set her up in a small home in a Detroit suburb and made sure that she and her baby were financially taken care of. Despite his light coloring, Barry grew up in a predominantly black neighborhood and he and his mother were well received.

Barry developed into a gregarious, intelligent and charming young man. His school grades were average, but his teachers considered him an under achiever. He was elected Student Body President in his senior year and although he secretly aspired to be voted 'Most Likely to Succeed', he good naturedly accepted the title of 'Most Likely to be the Best Used Car Salesman'.

Upon graduating high school, his grades were not good enough to qualify him to attend a four year university so he enrolled in the local community college. While attending classes there, his political science teacher recognized his quick wit and charm and convinced him to join the school's debating team where he met Paulo Santiago.

It was during debating competition that he began to appreciate fully his natural ability of persuasion and leadership and so did others. After his political science class one day, his instructor asked him to stay over.

"Brother Benjamin, I'd like to invite you to my apartment tonight. There are some people I'd like you to meet," he said, waiting for a reaction.

Wow, Barry thought. To be addressed as a Brother by one of his mentors was a big deal. He quickly composed himself and answered, "It'd be my pleasure, Brother."

That evening he was introduced to the leader and several others who belonged to a group called the 'Black Brotherhood'. It was explained to him that the group consisted of black business leaders, scholars and political organizers who were recruiting young black men with intelligence and potential leadership qualities to assimilate and further their cause.

If he swore allegiance to the 'Black Brotherhood' movement, they offered him a full scholarship and guaranteed entry to any university of his choice. Upon completing his education and with his loyalty to the brotherhood, his political ambitions would be unlimited.

Although his grades didn't warrant it, he was accepted into Harvard University where he did little to distinguish himself except being elected to President of the black student caucus. Upon earning his degree in black studies, he returned to Detroit and was given a high ranking job with the party's neighborhood political organizing committee.

Several years later he was elected a city Alderman and quickly developed a reputation of being an articulate orator as his aspirations grew. He met in back rooms with both union and management leaders of the automobile industry and after gathering enough political and monetary support, decided to run for the vacated U.S. Senate seat.

His landslide victory garnered him national prominence. A faction of the party leadership, who believed their presidential front runner could not be elected, approached him. Political pundits were astonished when this young, still in his first term, Senator was nominated by his party and was promptly elected the President of the United States. Barrymore Jasper Benjamin knew he was ordained and it was no surprise to him.

His reelection to a second term confirmed his opinion and he now sat about the job of changing the political structure of the nation that would enshrine his legacy. He already had the consensus of the Supreme Court and the U.S. Senate and now only needed the midterm elections in the House of Representatives to go his way and he could gain almost total Executive control.

It was just past midnight and he sat at his desk in the private office he had constructed off the Presidential Bedroom. The room was built like a large vault with the only access via a steel reinforced private door to his bedroom. The only other person besides himself who had been in that room was his Chief of Staff, Paola Santiago. Not even the cleaning staff was allowed entry and he personally kept the room neat and tidy.

His wife and two daughters were off in Colorado on a ski vacation and now sitting across the desk was Santiago.

"We know Rusk and his people are conducting their own investigation into locating this 'GWN'. How close are they?" the President asked.

"It's hard to say, sir. Since our man tailing that DOJ Inspector was ID'ed and we had to replace him, she's dropped off the grid. We think she was getting close and she's now working underground," Santiago replied.

He continued, "I believe we need to make a preemptive strike. The 'GWN' have served their purpose. Their trail of destruction has the general public up in arms, no pun intended. The latest polls indicate the voters support your gun legislation overwhelmingly."

"When you say a 'preemptive strike', do you mean we should conduct a Waco type assault? Hell, we don't even know where they are," the President exclaimed.

"Sir, these are the most hated and despised group of people since Osama Bin Laden and the Al Qaida. After we find them, and we will find them, by an Executive Order you can bring in our military and snuff this group in a nanosecond and except for a few grumblings from our chicken shit legislatures, nobody would dare second guess your decision. Hell, you'll be hailed as a hero," Santiago explained.

The President rubbed his chin and after a moment of thought, said, "Find out where they are. It's important we find them before Rusk's people do and, Paola, make sure our plan is not leaked. We need to be the ones to take credit for eliminating this menace."

"Yes. Mr. President," Santiago replied.

"And," the President continued, "When this is done, I hope you have a plan in mind to eliminate Rusk and his gang."

Santiago said with a wink, "Indeed, I have, sir."

—

CHAPTER TEN

Dinosa thought she was dreaming until she heard a gruff voice say, "Good job boys. Chain her to the wall in the cellar and I'll be down shortly. Thar's no reason for the others to know she's here."

She fought the urge to struggle and remained still as she was lifted and thrown over someone's shoulder. She still had a hood draped over her head and her legs were tied together at the ankles and her hands tied behind her.

She felt herself being carried down steps and heard a light switch turn on. She was laid gently down on some kind of a cot and her hands were untied. Again, she fought the urge to strike out and feigned unconsciousness as one wrist was shackled to a chain. Her feet were untied and the hood removed. Her eyes remained shut.

"She is a pretty little thang," one of her kidnappers said with a smirk.

"She's a Jezebel and don't you forget it," a large man with a white beard and a balding head in his early seventies roared as he descended the stairs. "When was the last time you stuck her?"

"About ten hours after we grabbed her, just like we were told, Joshua. That was about nine hours ago," the older of the two young men answered.

The older man walked over and leaned down to inspect his captive. He slapped her hard across her face and she did not respond, but thought to herself, this sorry mother fucker will regret he did that.

"She's still out. Come on up and have some supper with us and I'll send one of the women down to change her soiled britches."

As the group ascended the stairs they clicked off the light. Dinosa waited and listened for any movement in the room. Hearing none, she opened her eyes. It didn't take long for her vision to focus in the dark room. A bit of light shined through a storm window above her head and she could see it emanated from a porch light above the door to the home.

She looked around the room and could see the cot she lay on was in a corner of a large basement. In the corner of the room at the foot of the cot was a stairwell that disappeared above the ceiling. In the opposite side of the room she could make out a woodstove that she figured provided heat for the home. Firewood was stacked along the wall and she could make out some sort of a chute that she reasoned exited to the outside.

She reached over and grabbed the chain manacled to her left wrist and gave it a yank. To her surprise she thought, although in the darkness she couldn't see it, the wall anchor gave a little. She followed the chain with her fingers to the wall and found the square metal plate the chain was secured to. She yanked again and felt the plate again. She thought she felt a little, maybe a micro inch, gap between the plate and the wall.

Suddenly the overhead light came on and she quickly lay back down and closed her eyes. She heard someone descending the stairs. The footsteps approached and she knew it was two people.

"Oh, the poor girl," one voice said.

"Remember, Rachael, she is a Jezebel and a whore. Feel no pity for her," an older girl's voice said.

Dinosa felt someone sit down beside her and unclasp and unzip her slacks while another person slipped off her shoes. They pulled her pants down and then slipped off her panties.

'Oh shit,' Mary thought, 'here I am again in my nightmare where I'm the only naked one in the middle of the SFPD squad room.'

She felt a warm soapy sponge cleaning her privates and legs and then being toweled off. She chanced cracking one eye open as someone was slipping a pair of denim trousers over her feet. She was able to make out the face of the person struggling to put the pants on her. She was a homely girl, maybe sixteen or seventeen. Standing dutifully behind her was a pretty young girl she guessed to be several years younger holding a towel.

Dinosa closed her eye and the girl finally finished her chore. As she heard the girls leave she opened her eyes and watched them ascend and disappear up the stairwell. She rolled over and with her free hand adjusted her pants and felt them chafe her butt. 'Bitches couldn't give me a pair of panties?' she thought.

—

The five member team entered the Flying J diner and took a corner booth where they all ordered dinner. It was late afternoon and with the exception of the waitress and a few truck drivers sitting at the counter, they had the room to themselves.

"Okay, Ian and I are going to look up my old buddy and see what he can tell us. You guys are going to the Panhandle Gun and Outfitters Store and set up surveillance on the cousin, Claude Johnson," Chalmers said.

As dinner was served, Chalmers noticed one of the men sitting at the counter was sneering at them and said something to his partner. The only words Chalmers could make out was, "…Fucking nigger…"

Chalmers tensed and looked at Grant and then the rest of the team. They acted as if nothing had happened.

"Jesus, Grant, doesn't that bother you?" he asked.

Grant just shrugged and Jesse said, "It bothers all of us, but to react could compromise our mission, and we won't allow that."

"You guys are amazing," Chalmers said incredulously and added, "Grant, how does it make you feel that the people we are after would sooner kill you than look at you?"

Without looking up, Grant replied, "Probably the same way American Jewish soldiers felt fighting the Nazis in Europe during World War II."

—

After the two girls had left the basement, Mary realized how hungry and thirsty she was. How long had it been since she had any nourishment or liquids? She glanced around the room and noticed in the darkness a bottle of water and bowl of stew had been left beside the cot she lay on.

Despite her fears that if she drank the water and ate the food her captives would know she was awake, her natural urges won out. She first grabbed the bottle and slurped the water down and then devoured the bowl of stew. The stew she thought was quite tasteful and then chuckled at herself thinking she was so hungry a bowl of shit would have probably taste good.

The overhead light came on and three men trooped down the stairs. Leading the pack was a balding old man with a white beard wearing a plaid shirt and car hart overalls. He was followed by two younger men similarly dressed and bearded.

The older man pulled up a chair from the corner, positioned it next to and facing Dinosa and sat down. The other two men stood behind him.

In a pleasant voice, he said, "I see you enjoyed my wife's good cook'n. Now," he continued more menacingly, "You will answer my questions. What is your connection to Bernard Rusk?"

Mary tried to think how she should answer his questions. Shit, she'd never received any interrogation training except how to conduct one. She remembered old war movies and the response by captured U.S. soldiers.

"My name is Mary Dinosa. I'm a Special Investigator with the Justice Department and my Social Security number is..." she was interrupted by a hard slap that bloodied her lip.

She snapped her head back and glared at her attacker.

"You are not a POW! You are a whore! You are an adulterous harlot and you will eventually tell me what I want to know," the old man roared.

Dinosa continued to look at the old man with an insolent stare.

The old man stood up and walked to the other side of the room, stood next to a table and picked up a whip. Two wrist shackles hung from chains on the adjacent wall.

"Unshackle her and bring her here," the old man ordered.

One of the men reached in his pocket and produced a key. He walked over and bending over Dinosa he grabbed her free arm and started to insert the key in the wrist shackle.

Dinosa, now in a sitting position grabbed the man's forearm with her shackled hand, lunged forward and bit down on his arm as hard as she could.

"Bitch!" the man roared out in pain, and with Dinosa holding firm on her bite, he slammed the fist of his free hand into the side of her head. The blow bounced her head off the concrete wall and she slumped back onto the cot unconscious.

"Oh, God, did I kill her?" the man said, holding his bleeding arm.

The old man rushed across the room and looked down at Mary. Seeing she was still breathing, he said, "No, but you did put her out of commission for a while and you will do penance for your mistake."

He reached down and grabbed Dinosa by the jaw and turned her head to inspect her injuries. Deciding they were not life threatening, he said, "Come on upstairs, we'll continue this in the morning."

—

"Damn, it's good to see you, Chuck," Dwight Bradley MacArthur beamed as he threw his arms around Chalmers.

Ian stood behind Chalmers as they were greeted by Mack on his front porch.

"Come on in."

As they entered the front room, Chalmers turned to introduce his companion and said, "I'm not sure if you two have met, but this is Ian O'Farrell. Ian, this is Mack, the guy I used to be partnered with back in the SFPD."

Mack extended his hand and said, "No, we've never met, but I've heard all the rumors. You were quite the hero when Mary brought in the 'North Beach Murderer'."

"So, how did an old San Francisco flat foot end up the Police Chief of Bonners Ferry, Idaho," Chalmers asked, as they all took seats in the comfortable surroundings of Mack's living room.

"Well, my youngest son is an Idaho State Trooper assigned to this jurisdiction and when he heard the town was looking for a Chief, he called me.

"After I retired from the force, I was bored and decided to submit my application and viola, here I am. Four monthly alimony payments may have given me a little incentive," he chuckled.

A younger, slightly plump lady dressed in dark slacks and a silk blouse entered the room carrying a tray with three frosted mugs of beer.

"This is my new bride, Wanda," he said smiling proudly.

After introduction and small talk, she departed.

"Jesus, Mack, will you ever learn," Chalmers laughed.

"I'm living proof, you can't teach old dogs new tricks," Mack retorted with a giggle.

"So what brings you here and what can I do for you?" he asked.

"Mack, I hope it doesn't sound too patronizing when I say we can't get into details as to why we're here. I'm sure you have an idea of what we've been up to the last several years, so suffice it to say, we'll avoid doing anything that will jeopardize your position or interfere with your job. We just have some questions you might be able to help answer," Chalmers said.

"Chuck, quit blowing smoke up my ass. My job isn't like being the Chief of the SFPD, but I take it seriously and I've sworn to uphold and protect my citizens. Your presence here tells me you present a threat to that wellbeing. So, if you want my cooperation, you have to level with me," Mack said.

Chalmers look and Ian who nodded his assent and then said, "Okay, Mack, prepare yourself."

For the next hour, Chalmers and Ian explained their mission, starting with the Synagogue terrorist attack in San Francisco up to the present and answered Mack's questions forthrightly.

After they had concluded their presentation, Mack said, "Well, you know if they have Mary Dinosa, I'll do whatever I can to help. I've only been here a couple of months, but I do know the 'Panhandle Gun and Outfitters' shop and I'm acquainted with Claude Johnson.

"Let me tell you a little about the kind of folk that live up here. They're outwardly very friendly, but their private lives they believe are just that, private, and they're leery of people poking around, especially outsiders.

"Hell, if my boy hadn't lived here for several years and proved to be a good neighbor, they would never have accepted me. Some still don't. 'Don't Californicate Idaho' is more than a bumper sticker to these people.

"As far as my knowledge of any illicit clan activities in the area, these mountains are full of religious, white supremacy, alternative lifestyle, dope labs and any other type of compound you can think of. The courts have come down pretty hard on law enforcement when it comes to securing search warrants. They take their civil rights pretty seriously up here.

"I'll do some digging around and see what I can do. Chuck, I appreciate you coming clean with me and I understand the importance of your mission and that you may bend a few laws to accomplish it. I'll do whatever I can to help you, but as far as I'm concerned, tonight was just a couple of old city cops getting together and swapping lies about the good old days."

Rising to leave, Chalmers said, "You got it, and thanks for the beers. We'll be in touch."

As he and Ian departed through the front door, Chalmers turned and gesturing toward the kitchen, said with a chuckle, "See if you can hang on to this one."

—

The van pulled up and parked parallel and across the street from the Panhandle Gun and Outfitters store. Jesse glanced at his watch which read 1805 hours and said, "He doesn't close up for almost an hour."

The store was bigger than they thought it would be. The single story building with an adjacent parking lot took up better than half a block of the small town. The side walk windows were plaster with signs, one that read 'We Buy and Sell Used Guns', another that read 'Largest Selection of Rifles, Pistols and Ammo', and another that advertised 'Inquire Inside About Guided Hunts'.

"Man, they really must believe in self-protection in this town. The gun store is bigger than the grocery store," Grant commented.

"I don't think the home boys from the hood would do any drive byes in this town. Hell, even the little old ladies would be shooting back, forget about the cowboys," Jesse added.

"As a boy raised in Montana, let me pass on a little local wisdom to you fellows. Folks in these parts don't look at guns as something evil. Just like we learned in our military training, they look at their weapons as a friend, as a tool necessary to their survival. A rifle allows them to fill their freezers with meat and occasionally to fend off a predator, usually the four legged variety. Like you said, even the little old ladies will shoot the two legged ones, and that's a big deterrent.

"Per capita, there are more private gun owners in this part of the United States than any other place in the world and the least number of violent shootings," Chad explained.

"Yeah, well why do I get the idea they look at me as one of the two legged type?" Grant retorted.

"Oh, don't get me wrong. These are opinionated people, but the people native to these parts could give a shit what color you are as long as you mind your own business and behave. The race haters are mostly from the outside and move here to take advantage of our liberal gun laws and right to privacy. To most of the locals, they're not welcomed.

"Still and all, if I were you, I wouldn't be hittin' on any of the women," Chad concluded.

"I've spotted his vehicle," Jesse interrupted, peering through a pair of binoculars, and added, "It's the white Jeep Cherokee parked in the lot next to the rear door of the store. The license plate number confirms it."

"That's my cue," Chad said, exiting the side door of the van.

He walked to the corner, crossed the street and doubled back passed the store to the parking lot. Glancing around, he proceeded to stroll to the back of the Cherokee and as he passed the rear of the vehicle he stooped down and placed the small magnetized GPS transmitter device behind the bumper. He then continued across the lot and turned down an alley next to an adjacent establishment and disappeared.

A few minutes later he reappeared at the far corner and crossed the street and returned to the van.

Grant sat before a console in the cramped confines in the back of the van.

"Is it working?" Chad asked.

"Take a look," Jesse said, moving his head to allow Chad's view of the monitor.

The screen was filled with a satellite map of Bonners Ferry and showed a red illuminated dot where the Cherokee was parked in the lot off Main Street.

"Let's go find the farm house," Jesse said, sitting in the driver's seat and starting up the van

He found the on ramp to Highway 95 and they drove north out of town. The route followed the Kootenai River and the valley known for its' agricultural crops. The valley's soil produced everything from strawberries to the popular Idaho potatoes.

Approximately five miles later the van turned left onto an unmarked gravel road with just a mail box guarding its' entrance. The road cut straight through an alfalfa field and led them to a farm house located about two miles from the highway snuggled in a grove of black walnut trees at the eastern foot of the Cascade Mountain range.

Jesse parked the van in front of the porch and the men started unloading their gear. A motion detector lamp over the front door came on and illuminated the area as did another one located above the door of a barn across the yard.

The outside of the home looked like something out of the 'Andy Griffin Show' and the inside confirmed it. The front door entered into a large living room with a staircase that led upstairs, a hallway that led to the rear of the home and a door to the kitchen on the opposite side. Behind the staircase was a stairwell that descended to the basement.

In one corner of the living room sat a utility style desk stocked with the latest electronic equipment and a two-way radio. Jesse went immediately to the computer, booted it up and logged on to the 'Justice Foundation' isolated intra net system. He found the satellite map and the red dot indicating Claude was still at his store. He checked the audio and confirmed a rhythmic beeping would alert them when the vehicle was in motion.

Jesse remarked to no one in particular, "This is amazing. We get better support on these missions than we ever got during a military operation. Who the hell sat this up?"

"According to Ian this address was given to us by Bernard Rusk. He said something about it being an old safe house that was taken off the grid," Grant replied.

Jesse looked at Chad and asked, "You work for this man, Bernard Rusk. Who the hell is he and how did you get mixed up with him?"

"It's a long story and somewhat personal, but for what it's worth, Bernie is the most honorable man I know, and I've known a lot of honorable people," Chad said, sitting at the dining room table disassembling his hand gun and placing the pieces on a paper towel for cleaning.

The sound of another vehicle pulling into the driveway outside broke the ensuing silence. Grant pulled back the curtain and peeked out the front window. He watched as the SUV parked next to their van and Chalmers and Ian step out.

Entering the house, Ian looked around and said, "Not bad digs, very comfortable."

The team spent the next few minutes debriefing each other on their evening's activities and Jesse gave the group a dummy's course on how to operate the electronic equipment.

"We'll take three hour turns monitoring the map and I'll take the first shift. I suggest the rest of you get some shut eye," Chalmers said, taking the chair in front of the desk.

—

Mary lay on the warm beach with her head resting on Ian's chest. She could feel it rise and fall and hear the beating of his heart. He reached down and gently pulled her up and kissed her passionately. She could feel the lust building in his loins and she responded in kind. She thought herself in a romantic novel.

...Wait a second, she thought. I don't even like romantic novels! Her head started to pound with pain and she pushed herself away from Ian.

She opened her eyes and stifled a scream. She remembered her predicament and her body shivered with terror and her head throbbed with pain and the combination produced tears.

She tried to calm herself. Things could get worse, she thought, and then had to chuckle. You dumb bitch, how could things get any worse?

She couldn't remember where and by whom she had heard the phrase, 'Life is what happens while you're making other plans', and she chuckled to herself again at its' irony.

She tried to focus, but the light that had previously provided some light from the storm window was now extinguished and she found herself in total darkness. She remembered the shackle mount and how she thought she had budged it from the wall before she was interrupted.

She yanked the chain and then felt the mounting bracket. She felt a tiny crack between plate and the wall. She yanked several more times, each time feeling more pain emanate from her wrist. She felt the mount again and sensed the gap had widened, but only slightly. She realized her wrist would break before the shackle's anchor.

She needed a tool, she thought. Reaching under the cot she felt a support bar connected one of the legs to the bed frame. The bar was attached on either end by a single screw. She tried to remove one of them, but it was too small to grip with her fingers. She slid her finger nail into the screw's slot and only managed to break her nail. She needed a screwdriver, but doubted her captives would have left one within arm's reach.

She reached up and fingered a snap on her blouse. It might work, but how the hell could she remove it? She unsnapped her blouse and rolled over and felt something jab her in her ribs. She reached down and felt a metallic object. It felt like a key.

'Holy Mary, Mother of God!' It was a key. The dumb clod hopper must have dropped it when she bit the bastard's arm just before he knocked her into never, never land.

She slid the key into the slot of the wrist band and it sprung open. She removed her hand and gently rubbed her wounded wrist. The pain in her head subsided some as she reveled in her freedom. Then she realized she wouldn't be free until she was free from this dreadful place.

She rose and got off the cot and made her way quietly across the room to where she had spotted the wood chute earlier. She lifted the flap and calculated the size of the opening. It would be tight, but she thought she might fit. What if she got wedged and stuck? After contemplating what her fate might be if she stayed, she quickly dropped that thought.

She was about to start her journey up the chute when she heard someone unlocking the door at the top of the stairs. Grabbing the fire stoker rod that sat next to the woodstove, she darted back to the cot, replaced the shackle on her wrist and lay down with her back to the room with the rod grasped by her free hand and tucked underneath her as the light clicked on.

She heard footsteps of a person coming down the stairs. The man walked across the room and opened the woodstove door. He threw several logs on the fire and closed the door. He turned and walked toward Dinosa.

As he arrived at the cot, bending over he mumbled, "Where's that key?"

In one motion, Dinosa rolled over and with all her might swung the rod. It caught the man on the side of his head and with a groan he stumbled back. Dinosa leapt from the cot and swinging the rod from over her head landed a blow on the crown of the man's head which forced him to his knees. As if she was hitting a home run, with both hands grasping the rod she swung again. It connected to the side of the man's head and he fell to the floor, twitching in death spasms.

"I told you, you son of a bitch, you'd be sorry," she whispered.

She ran to the wood chute and opened the flap. She dropped to her knees and entered the chute. She found if she turned diagonally her shoulders would fit, but when her hips attempted to enter, the bulky denim trousers her captors had loaned her jammed. Shit, she thought.

She backed out of the chute and slipped out of the trousers. Thinking they would probably come in handy if she managed to scale the chute, she placed them ahead of her as she reentered.

The chute was slanted at about a forty-five degree angle and the going was slow. She was happy now that her wish for bigger boobs never materialized. Having no idea what time it was, her wish now was that the home's residents were fast asleep and the clod hopper wouldn't be immediately missed.

As she wiggled and shinnied her way up the shaft the air got cooler and the fact she knew she was making progress gave her hope. Finally the pants she was pushing became easier to move and then they popped out of the opening and she felt the rim of the chute with her leading hand. Pulling herself up and out of her confines she found herself in the wood shed. She made out a lamp hanging from the ceiling and dared to pull the switch string.

The light came on, temporarily blinding her. When she regained her sight she looked around. Half of the room was stacked with firewood. A hand ax lay against the stack. She put the trousers back on and put on a heavy wool jacket that was several sizes too big for her that she found hanging from the wall. She exchanged the stoking rod for the hand ax and cracked the door.

She saw the shed was attached to the rear of the house and no lights were on inside. She stepped outside and darkness surrounded her and she found herself standing in about a foot of snow. She had no way of knowing where she was, but knew she must be in the northwest and Ian and the team couldn't be too far from her.

She kept her distance from the house and circled it until she came to the freshly snow plowed road that led away from the home. Staying in the tree line where the snow was not as deep, she followed the road and crept silently.

After walking several hundred yards or so the sound of men talking stopped her in her tracks. She crept forward and as she got closer she could make out the silhouetted backs of two man entrenched in a bunker of some sort. The men wore military helmets and rifles were propped at each one's side.

She backed up and proceeded deeper into the woods, giving the men's position a wide berth. After plodding on for about another two miles or so she came to a paved and snow plowed road. She shivered in the cold trying to determine which way she should go.

She could see from the tree line that the geography appeared to go downhill to her left so she opted to go in that direction. Staying off the road and out of sight she made her way. The cold was becoming unbearable and her feet, shod in only socks and slip on shoes, were numb. Her head still pounded with pain, but she knew to stop moving would be disastrous.

She rounded a bend in the road and saw what had to be a house light across the road, maybe two hundred yards away. Praying these people were no comrades of her late captors, she made her way toward the light.

Approaching the home she noticed a hint of light on the horizon and she knew then she had been traveling east. She struggled up the steps to the front of the house and knocked weakly on the door.

A few minutes later a woman's voice asked, "Who is it?"

"Could you help me, please?" Mary heard herself say.

The door cracked opened and then swung open and an elderly woman cried, "My Lord, child! What's happened to you?"

Turning around she yelled, "Charlie, get out here and help!"

Dinosa, now shivering on her knees, looked up and said pitifully, "Thank you, ma'am."

—

The two men sat hunched down in the tree line and watched as the ambulance with lights flashing pulled into and down the driveway. It stopped in front of the house and a man and a woman jumped out and disappeared inside carrying a stretcher. A moment later a Bonner's Ferry police cruiser pulled in behind the ambulance and a large man jumped out and ran up the stairs and in the front door.

One of the two men, hiding in the trees, depressed the send button on his two way radio and described the scene.

A voice came back, "Return to base."

Inside the home the bulky police officer found Dinosa on a bed in the rear of the home. The female EMT was bandaging her head and the male attendant was preparing an IV. The elderly couple was standing at the head of the bed, the woman holding Dinosa's hand.

Dinosa jerked her arm away as the male attendant reached for it and slurred through swollen lips, "You ain't sticking me with that!"

"Dinosa, you sure haven't mellowed much with age," the police officer said.

She looked over to see who had said that, blinked her eyes, leaned forward and moaned, "Jesus Christ, I gotta be dreaming. Is that you Mack?"

"I can tell you you're not dreaming," Mack remarked.

"Holly shit...I mean, how the hell did you?...What the hell is going on?"

"I'm your knight in shining armor."

"Fuck you, Mack, and tell this big palooka he's not gonna stick me with that needle!"

"Son, if you cherish your balls, I'd listen to the lady," Mack said.

"But Chief, it's protocol," the young EMT protested, and then looking at the snarl on Dinosa's face, simply shrugged and rolled up the IV tubing and stowed it in his bag.

"You are a sight for sore eyes," Mack said.

Dinosa suddenly became aware of how she must look. Her head was wrapped in bandages and she knew her lips and probably one eye were swollen and she wore an old robe the lady of the house had loaned her.

She sat up and realized her entire body was aching and sore and winced, "Mack, it's imperative that I get a hold of Chalmers. Can I borrow your phone?"

"Don't worry Mary. I've already talked to him and he and Ian are meeting us at the hospital," Mack said.

"Hospital, I ain't going to the fucking hospital!" she exploded, painfully jumping up.

"Sir, I'm afraid it's mandatory," the young EMT pleaded.

"John, if you ever want to make babies, I'd back down," Mack said with a chuckle.

"Ma'am, if I could borrow some appropriate clothing, I'd gladly pay you handsomely," Dinosa said, looking at the elderly woman.

"Oh child, don't be silly," the woman replied, scurrying out of the room.

When the woman returned with the clothes the group left the room to allow Dinosa privacy to get dressed. Mack gathered them in the living room and said, "Charlie, Martha, I appreciate what you've done for my old friend," and looking at the two EMTs he added, "And John and Barbara, you've done an excellent job and I apologize for your, should we say, uncooperative patient, but I'm going to ask all of you to keep this incident under your hats. For the safety of this young lady, it's imperative that no one knows about it."

Looking at John, he said, "Can you dummy your call report to reflect that it was a minor injury to Charlie or Martha?"

John nodded and Charlie said, "Our lips are sealed."

—

"Well, they're gonna know where we are now," Joshua said to the group of men gathered in a grotto they called 'Operations HQ'.

Looking at his captain, he added, "Moses, double the perimeter security and gather the women and children and put them in the community center."

Turning to another of his followers he said, "Jed, get your team and load the package and be prepared to depart in an hour. You know our holy mission, just the time table has changed. People, Armageddon is upon us!"

—

Daniel 'Grub' Tanaka sat at the terminal connected to the 'Justice Foundation' isolated intranet he had set up and programmed. Means of communication was linked to a satellite signal provided by Bernard Rusk and was impossible to hack.

When he told Rusk what he needed, he was surprised when the reply was, "No problem."

Rusk had appropriated an entire CIA COMSAT (communications satellite) for the sole use by the foundation. Any electronic device required a proprietary V chip produced by Grub to receive and send digital information. Every member, plus Rusk, had the programmed V chip installed in their electronic devices. The system allowed information and communication to be shared between individuals or intranet wide.

Grub turned to the others in the lab and excitedly said, "Good news, everybody. Mary Dinosa escaped and is fairly healthy and back in the fold."

Snoopy and Teddy dropped what they were doing and rushed to look at Grub's monitor.

"There's more..." Grub said.

Another memo appeared on the screen from Bernard Rusk.

Congratulations on the safe return of Mary. Also, I want to give everyone a heads up. We have released some confidential internal State Department and Interior Department memos to most of the media outlets that will prove very embarrassing to the White House.

It is our hope that this action will disrupt or at least delay White House interference in our current mission. God speed to all of you.

That afternoon on a FOKS News Network daily talk show the host was saying;

...We've invited Robert McCormick, former Deputy Interior Secretary under the Bush Administration, on the show to help explain what these newly released inter Whitehouse memos mean. Mr. McCormick, what do you make of these memos?

"I think they lay out the President's and his people's real strategy behind his gun control agenda. It tells us they are prepared to go to any measures to rewrite the Constitution's Second Amendment and take the guns away from all law abiding citizens.

It also lays down his plan to establish through Executive order his own private police force and deputizing members of the Black Brotherhood in leadership positions of that force."

—

CHAPTER ELEVEN

"God damn it Paulo, how in the hell did those memos get leaked!?" President Benjamin yelled.

"Mr. President," Santiago began, knowing it was times like this that he show his deference and stroke his boss's ego, "The question should be, now that these memos have been leaked, how do we spin it?"

"And how, pray tell, do we do that?" the President barked sarcastically, pushing his chair back from his desk in the Oval Office.

"First, we don't directly respond to these allegations, at least not now, and we tell the memo recipients to do the same. We tap our media resources and spin doctors to question the sources of the leaks. They can say these are the same people that lied to the citizens of the United States when they told us that Iraq had weapons of mass destruction and sent this nation to war under false pretenses.

"I'm sure we can find people at the FBI Electronic Forensic Unit to question the validity of the memos and the possibility that they were covertly planted.

"When the time is right, you can claim deniability and we can establish the fact that your enemies have conspired to bring you down. You can express your outrage that some people would so corruptly circumvent the good you have accomplished.

"How do we deal with Rusk and his people?" the President asked, a bit more calmly.

"Well, they're obviously the ones behind this. We've identified at least seven others who have conspired with him. Unfortunately their numbers and their positions and knowledge alone means we can't eliminate them now so we need to discredit them. We're conducting that investigation and developing a plan to do just that.

"The most important thing at this time, Mr. President, is we don't panic."

—

The entire team was assembled in the front yard as the police cruiser pulled up and stopped. Ian opened the passenger door and stretched an arm to help Dinosa out.

She pushed his arm away and snapped, "For Christ's sake, I can get out of a fucking cop car on my own."

Ian leapt back to the nervous laughter of everyone. Chalmers was roaring with laughter and paused long enough to say, "Same old Mary, it's great to see you haven't lost your gross sense of humor."

"Ah shit," she said seriously and then smiled broadly and slurred through her swollen lips, "Whenever Chalmers calls me by my first name, my asshole automatically puckers."

She winced and added, "It only hurts when I smile."

Ian led Mary up the stairs and the group followed them into the house. He escorted her to a back bedroom and she sat down on the bed. He picked up a pill and a glass of water from the bed side table and handed them to her, saying, "I can't wait to hear every detail of your little adventure, but you need some sleep. Take this and I'll check on you later."

"Ian, I need you to promise me, when the shit hits the fan, I'll be there."

"You got it," Ian said, closing the door gently behind him.

When he returned to the living room, everyone was either looking at their I-pads or laptops and Jesse was sitting at the desk observing the computer monitor. Ian walked to his back pack and retrieved his lap top and patched into the satellite imagery everyone else was observing.

The voice communication was turned on and they heard Rusk say, "Well boys, there's your target."

Jesse depressed a key on his computer and the image appeared on the 80" large screen television located in a corner of the room. Everyone's attention turned toward it.

The live broadcast showed an aerial view of a two story home butted up to a cliff that rose to mountains. From the projected shadows it was obviously a southern view. A gravel road could be seen going north from a paved road to the home. The camera was slowing moving north with the home as its focal point.

"Holy crap," Ian exclaimed, "We didn't even have this kind of surveillance when we got OBL. Who the hell is maneuvering the satellite?"

"That's need to know information, Commander," Rusk said and continued, "It'll take about an hour to scan the entire compound."

The group watched in silence. The images showed the compound was guarded by an outside and inside perimeter. About a mile up the gravel road it was protected on either side by bunkers manned with two armed sentries in each. Another mile up the road and about two hundred yards from the house was a steel gate and what looked like a ten foot cyclone fence topped with razor wire that extended on either side of the gate to the cliff behind the house.

The silence in the room was broken when Grub's voice came over the intercom.

"They're going to have a sophisticated surveillance system. You're going to need me and Snoops to hack it and we'll have to be on sight," he said calmly.

"I've already looked it up and the Boundary County Airport can't accommodate anything larger than a fixed winged twin engine airplane. We can take my plane and our ETA at Bonners Ferry will be about four hours after takeoff. Can you and Snoops meet me at Novato Municipal Airport in an hour?" Sol Goldsmith interrupted.

"We'll be there," it was Snoopy.

—

Corky Burmeister peeked out from behind the curtain hoping because the news conference had been hastily called she would only see a few cameras and a scattering of media people.

She audibly moaned when she saw the room was overcrowded and people were setting up cameras and taking lighting tests while others were tapping their microphones and making final airing preparations.

She remembered how proudly five years ago she had accepted the appointment as the President's Press Secretary. She delighted in the challenge of controlling the situation and spinning her answers to conform to the President's agenda. She knew she was good at her job and quick on her feet.

She remembered how enthralled she had become as a second year journalism student at the University of Michigan when Barry Benjamin was a guest lecturer at her political science class and how moving his lecture had been. Upon graduation she joined his political awareness committee and took a day job as a cub reporter with the Detroit Daily News.

Now, after hitching her tail, in more ways than one, and following him as he rose the party ranks to U.S. Senator and now the President, she was having misgivings. What the hell was going on, she wondered? Had she been made the fool all these years? How long can she go on telling half-truths and outright lies in order to justify his agenda? Is it just blind naivety on her part?

It had been weeks since their last romantic tryst and except for the occasional morning briefings, she'd had little contact with him. He wasn't even at the briefing for the today's press conference. It was just Santiago and herself. They went over an exhaustive series of questions she might be asked and how she should answer them.

Her job was to look confidently into the eyes of the questioners and tell them what she had rehearsed and mostly being evasive. She had done this so many times before, but now she questioned whether she could do it again. God, she thought, why didn't I just gracefully resign like so many other staff members and department heads after Barry's first term?

A young man holding a clipboard scurried past her and said, "You're up in five, Corky."

Suddenly she felt light headed and nauseated. She looked frantically around for a waste paper basket and before she could find one, her half-digested breakfast erupted from her stomach and spilled onto the floor, her shoes and her blouse.

A few minutes later a young spokesman strolled to the podium and said, "I'm sorry people, but Ms. Burmeister has taken ill and is unable to conduct the news conference. We will reschedule it as soon as possible and let you know."

He walked off the stage to the moans of those gathered, leaving them to wonder, what the hell is going on?

—

It was dark outside and a light snow was falling when the van driven by Grant and carrying Snoopy, Grub and Sol pulled in and parked in front of the farm house. They unloaded their overnight bags and trudged up the stairs and into the home.

Greetings, hugs and handshakes were exchanged and Chalmers introduced Chief MacArthur to the newcomers. Dinosa emerged from a bathroom down the hall and joined the group. She was freshly showered with her hair pulled back into a pony tail under a baseball cap. Her right eye and cheek were swollen and bruised and her upper lip was slightly puffed bearing a slight split. A white band aid patch protruded from under the cap on her left forehead and above her ear.

Upon entering the room, Snoopy's jaw dropped and rushing toward her she cried, "Oh my God, Mary, what happened to you?"

She gently hugged Dinosa, who replied, "It's good to see you too, Snoops, and thanks for such a flattering greeting."

"I'm so sorry, Mary," Snoopy said sincerely.

"That's okay, Snoops," Dinosa said smiling and touching her sore lip. "It is good to see you. I'm sure it looks worse than it is."

Ian interrupted and said, "Why don't you guys stow your gear. Snoopy, we've prepared a room at the end of the hall for you and Grub. Sol, Mack here has graciously offered a room at his house. It's only a few miles away. We're getting a little crowded here.

"We've edited and digested the video we've received today and were about to review it in a strategy planning meeting. Please join us."

Jesse dragged in several chairs from the dining room and placed them in front of the large screen television to accommodate the late arrivals and he then took a chair next to the video controls.

For the next two hours they observed the video, freezing it and using the zoom capability when anyone requested. Portions were scrolled forward and backward and scrutinized from various angles as the satellite imagery scanned over the compound.

Grub cleared his throat and said, "From what I observed, they have an extensive and sophisticated video surveillance system. I counted at least fifteen cameras located throughout the compound. They have to be negated if your plan is to assault the facility."

"What do you need?" Chalmers asked.

"Firstly, I'll have to be on sight. I have the equipment to intercept their broadcast frequency and I can hack it, but it will that require I have a clear line of sight to each camera," Grub replied.

"Just a second," Jesse said.

He brought up on the television one of the last frames of the video that was taken from the north and showed the entire compound from slightly behind the cliff. With a laser pen he pointed out a spot located at the top of the cliff and the start of the tree line.

"Would this location suffice?" he asked.

"That would be excellent," Grub said with a smirk.

"We still don't have an accurate count of how many people live in the compound. We do believe they've accepted no outsiders, but considering they started with four or five couples and they've lived here for over forty years, Grub estimates their present population could be as many as one hundred fifty with approximately a third of that number under the age of sixteen.

"We've identified three entrances to caves dug into the cliff behind the home. Based on the people movements we think the entrance on the left must access their living quarters, the one in the center their religious and military center, and the large entry on the right must be their munitions and supply depot," Chalmers said.

"Mary, can you add anything?" Ian asked.

"I'm afraid not. My main objective was to get the hell out of there. I stumbled upon one of those bunkers, but it was too dark to make out any details, except they were armed with rifles and outfitted in combat gear. Their security is set up to keep people out not in."

"Did anyone of them say anything that may be helpful?" Ian persisted.

"Well, the leader called me a Jezebel and a whore, well actually a harlot, and he made several other Biblical references. He looked to be at least seventy years old and a resurrected Moses. These people are not only a hate group but also a bunch of religious fanatics. That's a bad ass combination," Dinosa concluded.

Suddenly the front door swung open. Everyone in the room with a sidearm instinctively reached for it.

"What kind of a security system is this?" Steve Cromwell said, stomping the snow off of his boots.

Nancy followed him into the room.

"Jesus Christ, what are you guys doing here?" a surprised Grant said with some relief.

Nancy replied, removing her knitted cap and shaking her hair out, "You didn't think we'd miss this party, did you?"

"It's good to see you guys. Come on in, we'll make room for you somewhere," Chalmers said, greeting Steve with a handshake and Nancy with a hug.

"Not to worry," Steve said, "We drove our RV over and we're self-contained."

The group spent the next hour briefing Steve and Nancy and they watched a quick review of the video.

Nancy walked over to Jesse and said, "May I have the remote, please."

Jesse handed her the video remote and she brought up the frame that showed where Grub would locate his equipment. She moved the cursor over two small objects located at the apex of the cliff and zoomed in. The enlarged frame showed two hooded pipes approximately four inches in diameter and extending up about a foot from their granite bases.

"Those look like intake and return vents to an air circulation system to me," she said.

The room fell silent until Sol stammered, "That's amazing, how in the hell did you spot them?"

"Because military policy does not allow the weaker sex in combat positions," Nancy stated sarcastically and then continued, "My job with the team was FO, or forward observer. In Afghanistan and Pakistan, identifying vents like these is how we located enemy caves. I spotted two other vent locations here."

She returned to the original video frame and pointed out the other two locations.

Chad looked up in the air and asked loudly, "Bernie, are you still with us?"

"Ten-four," a voice replied.

"Can you get us some canisters of MAX gas?"

"It'll be delivered within twenty-four hours."

"What the hell is MAX gas?" Mack asked.

"It's' a mixture of carbon monoxide, alcohol and the X stands for some military secret compound. Its' a nonlethal gas that quickly knocks out anyone breathing it. A person's first reaction after inhaling it is like a euphoric drunk and within a minute its' never, never land," Grant explained.

"How long will it last?" Mack asked.

"About an hour after it's administered. As long as a person is exposed the longer he'll be in dreamland."

"Any side effects?"

"Oh, a slight headache and hang over is experienced by most people. I suppose it's' like a hangover after a drinking binge and it affects people differently." Grant said, hoping his explanation was enough.

"Okay people, they know we know where they are, so we'll have to move quickly. I think we will all agree this has to be an after dark mission. Let's set a tentative zero hour as sun down the day after tomorrow. In the interim, everyone review the material we went over this evening and we'll formulate our final plan over the next few days," Ian said.

—

CHAPTER TWELVE

President Benjamin sat behind his desk in the Oval Office perusing the letter with his reading glasses perched low on his nose and a scowl on his face. He looked up and across the desk at Corky Burmeister.

"Are you serious?" he snarled.

"Barry, I've just had enough. I can't take it anymore. I'm burnt out," Corky moaned as a tear ran down her cheek.

His tone changed and he pleaded, "But Corky, what about the years we've been together? You've been my rock and I love you. What about the life we've planned together after I'm out of this wretched office and I can get a divorce?"

"This doesn't have to change our plans," Corky sniveled and continued, her voice getting louder, "I'm in love with you, but I just can't continue with this façade. I feel like a hypocrite dodging the hard questions and putting on the spin. I'm not built that way and for my own sanity, I need to get out!"

"Okay, okay, calm down Corky," the President said in comforting tones and added as he stood up, "Just let me rewrite your letter of resignation. It is a sensitive situation."

"Fine," she replied.

Moving around the desk to her side, he lifted her up by her arms and kissed her passionately.

"When can I see you again," he whispered in her ear.

"I'll be at home tonight," she replied demurely.

"I'll call you later."

After Corky departed he returned to his desk and depressed the button on his intercom and gruffly said, "Miss Albright, get Paulo in here ASAP."

—

"Will, wake up! What's that sound?" the elderly woman said nudging her husband who was lying next to her buried under blankets and a bed quilt.

"Huh, huh?" he said rolling over and still half asleep.

"Listen, what's that sound?" the woman said.

Will propped himself up on an elbow and strained to hear. From the distance he could hear a diesel engine that seemed to be getting louder and approaching their cabin which was located half way up Squaw Mountain in the eastern Cascades Mountain Range.

He got out of bed and slipped on his wool socks that lay next to the bed and then shuffled to the bedroom window and pulled back the shades. A light snow was falling on the already three foot accumulation of the white stuff.

"Beats me, Gretchen, can't be a loggin' truck, they won't be back 'til spring."

Gretchen joined him, standing behind and looking over his shoulder. A set of headlights appeared rounding a bend in the road and coming up the mountain. Their cabin sat about fifty yards off the road.

"Looks like one of them snow tractors," Will said.

"Probably looking for some lost or stranded cross country skiers. You'd think those nature people would have more sense," Gretchen said disgustedly.

"Well, that thing might pack the snow down enough so we can get to town in the morning," Will said, looking at the bright side as the snow tractor whizzed by and disappeared around the next corner of the switch backed road.

Inside the tractor's cab, Jesse exclaimed, "Jesus Grant, ain't you going a little fast?"

"Quit crying like a little girl. If I can operate an Abram's tank, driving this is like a walk in the park. Remember, I flew us out of Mexico," Grant retorted.

Thinking back to that harrowing experience, Jesse turned and looking at Steve in the back of the cab, moaned, "Oh shit, we're in big trouble. If I remember correctly, he didn't land the plane."

After traveling several more miles up the road, which at times was difficult to distinguish, Grant stopped the tractor and announced, "It looks like we're on foot from here."

Steve consulted his GPS and said, "Well, we've got about a two mile hike."

They donned white nylon parkas and ski pants and gathered their gear. Once outside, they attached snow shoes to their boots and began their journey.

About an hour later they came to the crest of the ridge and proceeded downhill until they reached the tree line where they put on their night vision goggles. Here the landscape fell off sharply and they could see where the cliff began.

"According to the GPS, the middle vent should be right below us and the other two about one hundred feet on either side of us. I'll anchor a piton here and you two can maneuver and place yours accordingly," Steve said.

The men stowed their gear, which included rappelling ropes and harnesses, the canisters of MAX gas, and Grubs electronic equipment, on the ground above the tree line.

Jesse and Grant then disappeared in either direction and Steve inched his way down the steep incline until he came to the granite surface at the top of the cliff, the valley floor some two hundred feet below. There he anchored his pitons and made his way back up to the tree line where he waited for his companions to begin the trek back to the tractor.

Back at the farm house Chad wandered out of his bedroom and down the hall to the front room that was now empty except for Ian who sat at the desk manning the monitors and writing on a tablet.

"Hey Ian, "he said in a low voice, "I just got a telephone call from my FBI connection."

Ian stopped writing and looked up.

Chad continued, "He just received orders from his boss to mobilize his entire field agent force. They've been ordered to rendezvous at the National Guard Armory in Coeur d' Alene, Idaho, and await further orders. He says his counterpart at ATF received the same order. Something's up."

Ian took a moment to think and then said, "Coeur d' Alene is only a two hour drive from here. They must have found out at least the vicinity of where the GWN is. It shouldn't take them long now to pin point their location. If we want to conduct a preemptive strike, we'll have to move up our timetable."

"I'm sure you've figured out that a frontal attack could be disastrous," Chad said and added, "We don't have the fire or man power for that."

"I know that, Chad, we need to get inside. That's where our old friend Claude could come in handy," Ian said with a smirk.

—

"Now Mister Johnson, be reasonable. We know they're somewhere in northern Idaho or Montana and you know exactly where this Great White Nation is. Just tell us and we'll go away," Al Long pleaded.

He was standing in front of a man tied to a chair in the man's basement of his country home outside the town of Hayfork, Arkansas. To his right sat his family, his wife and five children from the ages of eight to sixteen, all bound to chairs, blind folded and gagged. They were moaning and sweating profusely.

"I ain't telling you shit," Johnson spat out defiantly.

Long nodded at his companion standing next to the oldest sibling, the Johnson's sixteen year old son. A pistol was aimed at the boy's head. He pulled the trigger and the resulting explosion in the small confines was ear shattering. Blood from the exit wound sprayed onto his younger sister sitting next to him who squealed in terror. The man took a step forward, cocked the gun and aimed it at her head.

"Aaaaaaah, noooooo!" Johnson's scream echoed off the walls. "You mother fucker!"

"Where are they?" Long repeated calmly.

"All right, I'll tell you!"

After Johnson showed him on a map where he could find the GWN, Long and his companion executed the entire family and left the residence.

PART III

THE BATTLE

"Surprise, speed and stealth are the elements one needs for success on the battle field."
General Norman Schwarzkopf, Jr.

CHAPTER THIRTEEN

The President, his Chief of Staff, the U.S. Secretary Attorney General along with his assistant, the U.S. Director of Homeland Security and the U.S. Secretary of Defense along with one of his senior advisors, were crowded around a table in the White House Situation Room.

"Our intelligence has located the headquarters and compound of the Great White Nation," the President began. "The question now, is how do we proceed?"

Paulo Santiago was the first to respond, "Whatever you decide to do, Mister President, we have to act quickly and decisively. We can't afford the luxury of time. This information is bound to leak out and that could prove disastrous."

He continued, "The Attorney General has already ordered a number of FBI and ATF agents to a bivouac area in Coeur d' Alene, Idaho, and is equipping them with SWAT and combat gear. An assault plan has already been formulated and is contained in the folder before all of you. I'm not sure this is the most optimum plan. We don't need another 'Waco' to deal with."

The Secretary of Defense, as he thumbed through the material before him, said, "How did we come by this material?"

The Director of Homeland Security blustered and said, "The information was gathered by my bureau. Our methods, of course are confidential, but I can assure everyone the information is one hundred percent reliable."

"I think we should consider a drone strike on the compound," Santiago said, pushing his chair back and clasping his hands behind his head.

"Are you nuts?" the Secretary of Defense said incredulously. "We can't conduct a military operation on our own citizens in our own country!"

"A precedent has already been set," the Homeland Security Director argued and continued, "We've conducted similar operations on U.S. citizens determined to be terrorists all over the world."

"And those decisions have created controversy and criticism from all sides. Hell, its being discussed in our Congress as we speak," the Defense Secretary retorted.

"The American people demand action! For Christ's sake, to term these people as 'citizens' is tantamount to calling Judas a Jew! The people of the United States don't care how we eliminate these animals, they just want them eliminated," Santiago roared and concluded, saying "Hell, the President will be hailed as a hero!"

"Can we do it," the President asked calmly.

"It'll take some planning," the Homeland Security Director said. "We can launch the drones from Utah and be over the target within a couple of hours. I think it should be a night time attack. The cover of darkness will minimize the threat of media coverage and disrupting the lives of innocents living in the area."

"How soon can we begin the attack?" Santiago asked.

"Tomorrow night," the Homeland Security Director replied and added, "The FBI and ATF agents on the ground can conduct the cleanup action, if any is necessary."

"I want to go on record as opposing any of this," the Defense Secretary sighed.

The President looked at his Homeland Security Director and said, "I want the complete battle plan on my desk by five tonight. You realize, Charlie, if this goes south, it will rest on your shoulders."

"I accept that," the Director replied.

As the group dispersed President Benjamin motioned toward Santiago and said, "Paulo, stick around for just a minute."

When they were left alone he said, "Corky Burmeister has become a problem. She handed in her letter earlier this morning."

He handed Paulo the letter and continued, "I rewrote it and had her sign it, but her state of mind is really fucked up and she's become a liability."

"She'll be home tonight and expecting me," he said, handing Paulo a key. "Make sure its quick and looks like a suicide, will you?"

"You got it, Mister President."

—

A light cold rain was falling as Al Long turned onto Cherry Lane off of the Plank Highway just outside the village of Spotsylvania, Virginia, about thirty miles south of the Capitol. A block and a half later he pulled into the parking lot of a townhouse condominium development, parked by the entrance and checked the time. The digital readout on his dashboard clock read 12:20 am.

He opened the knapsack sitting on the passenger seat and examined the contents. He pulled out a pair of tight fitting leather gloves and slipped them on. He then removed a twenty-two semiautomatic pistol, checked to make sure the clip was full, chambered a round and attached a silencer. He pulled out a five foot piece of rope and tested the slip knot. Putting on a black ski mask, he slipped out of the car, secured the hand gun between his trousers and the small of his back, picked up the knapsack and walked toward the townhouse at the far end of the first building.

From the outside the house was dark except for a dim light glowing from an upstairs bedroom. He glanced around to ensure he wasn't seen and then slipped the key into the door knob and slowly opened the front door.

"Is that you, Barry? I'm upstairs wearing your favorite teddy and I've planned something special for you tonight," Corky yelled down in her sexiest voice.

Al smiled under his mask and thought, so our President is a kinky sort. He made his way up the stairs, pausing at the top to tie one end of the rope to the landing's rail. He produced the handgun and proceeded to Corky's bedroom and swung it open.

"Come on in, big boy," Corky purred.

He looked around confused and perplexed. No one was there. He ran to the closet and flung it opened. No one was there either.

Behind him he heard Corky say, "Tell that son of a bitch I'm going to nail his balls to the wall."

He whirled around to an empty room.

"What the...?" he started to say when he spotted the camera and speaker on the bedside table.

He frantically fled the room, untied and gathered the rope tied to the railing, ran down the stairs and out the front door.

Two apartments over, Corky peeked through the window of the darkened living room and watched the masked man run across the parking lot, jump in his car and speed away.

She turned facing her neighbor and with a quaking voice said, "Beatrice, thank you so much for your hospitality."

Beatrice sat on the couch in front of a computer monitor with her mouth agape. Finally she said, "Jesus Christ, Corky, you certainly had a right to be paranoid. Who was that guy and whose balls are you going to nail to the wall?"

"I don't know," Corky lied. "Could I borrow your phone and have some privacy, please?"

Beatrice handed her a cordless phone and left the room. Corky removed an address book from her purse and thumbed through it. She dialed a number with trembling fingers.

After numerous rings the other end picked up.

"Hello?" a sleepy male voice answered.

"Mister Rusk, this is Corky Burmeister, I'm..."

"I know who you are, Miss Burmeister. How did you get my home phone number?" Rusk asked annoyingly.

"It's listed on the EOB. I'm sorry, that stands for Enemies of Barry and was put together by Paulo Santiago and was distributed to several of us at the White House."

Rusk couldn't restrain a chuckle and said, "That makes sense. What can I do for you, Miss Burmeister?"

Corky related the events of the day and included the fact that she had an ongoing affair with the President for the last ten years. She finished by saying, "I'm frightened to death and I don't know what to do. I was hoping you could help."

Rusk thought for a moment and then asked where she was. When she told him, he paused again and then said, "Stay where you are. The Spotsylvania Police Chief is a friend of mine. He'll have a squad car pick you up in less than a half an hour and transport you to Police Headquarters. I'll arrange for a friend of mine to pick you up there in a couple of hours. Do everything he says and you'll be safe. Do you understand?"

"Yes, Mister Rusk, and thank you."

—

"Holy Shit, you fucking moron! How could you fuck this up?" Santiago roared into his phone.

"Paulo, I don't particularly like your tone," Al Long snarled sarcastically and menacingly from the other end, and added, "Don't forget you did the planning for this and more importantly, do not forget to whom you are talking."

There was a pause and apologetic Santiago replied, "Yes, yes, of course you're right and I'm sorry. The most important thing now is how to find her. Do you have any suggestions?"

"Well, I did notice the monitor was wireless, so that means she had to be fairly close to receive and broadcast. If I were you, I'd get a team over there ASAP to observe the complex. She can't stay hidden forever," Long said.

"Where are you now? Can't you get back there and observe until I can get some of our people there?" Santiago pleaded.

"Sorry Paulo, but I'm going to opt out of this one. If you find her, you know how to get a hold of me and I might opt back in," Long said before the line went dead.

—

"I have good news and bad news," Ian said, setting another platter of flap jacks next to a pan of bacon on the dining table where the entire team was present, plus Sol Goldsmith and a bruised but surprisingly sprite Mary Dinosa.

"The good news, please," Nancy requested.

"Well, we've finalized the plan and it looks pretty good. Grub would probably calculate it at a fifty-fifty chance for success," Ian said smiling.

A roar went up from the attendees.

Dinosa looked quizzically around the room and smirked, "Who the fuck are you people? Do you realize that also means we have a fifty-fifty chance of failure?"

Grant chuckled and remarked, "If Grub would give it fifty-fifty, we'd bet our last dime on the spread and win."

"Okay, I give, what's the bad news?" Dinosa sighed.

"We have to move up our time line and strike tonight and the weather calls for overcast skies so we won't have the real time video," Ian said, soaking a fork full of flap jack in his syrup.

"That ain't such bad news," Jesse said.

"Eat up, everybody, we'll go over the plan and our individual assignments after breakfast," Ian said, taking a bite of crisp bacon.

Dinosa gazed around the room at her friends and just shrugged.

—

Colleen and her daughter, Jennifer, sat at the breakfast table. Colleen was sipping a cup of coffee and Jennifer was slurping down the last kernels of her oat bran cereal.

"Do you think Pop will be home for Christmas? You know it's only a few days away," Jennifer asked.

"Well, you know you're his favorite daughter, so I'm sure he'll make every effort to be here for you," Colleen replied with a smile.

"Mom, I'm his only daughter! Does that mean I'm also his least favorite daughter?" she giggled.

"Probably both," Colleen said and changing the subject, added, "What are your plans for the day?"

"Matt and Sheila and her new boyfriend are picking me up later this afternoon and we're going to catch a late matinee at the Alhambra Theater and then probably drive out to the Marina Green and neck in the back seat."

"Jennifer Lee Chalmers, you're incorrigible!" her mother groaned in mock horror. "Just make sure you're home by eleven."

—

Gretchen dropped her knitting on her lap, leaned back in her easy chair rocker, pulled back the curtain behind her and peered out the window.

As the snow tractor sped by, she said, "There they go again."

Her husband Will remained undisturbed, asleep in his recliner.

—

Claude Johnson checked his wrist watch which told him it was 7:02 pm. He removed his apron and laid it across the counter and walked to the front door and locked it and turned the 'closed' sign hanging on the door.

Alone in his store, he proceeded back to the counter and entered the stock room where he turned off the front lights. Crossing the stock room to the rear door, he armed the alarm, opened the door and switched off the remaining lights. He closed and locked the door behind him and walked to and got into his van.

Before he started the vehicle he reached under his seat and produced a pint of Jack Daniels whiskey and took a long swig, anticipating his stop at the Bonner Gentlemen's Club on his way home.

Replacing the bottle, he inserted a key into the ignition and started the van. He was about to place the gear shift in reverse when he felt the muzzle of a gun pressed against his temple and a voice that said, "Move, yell or do anything stupid and you're a dead man, understand?"

Claude's mouth fell open and his eyes widened as he simply nodded and said, "If you're gonna rob me, you can have it all. There's money in the store till too."

"We're not here to rob you, but we will kill you if you don't do everything I say. Are you a hero, Claude?" Ian asked menacingly.

Claude shook his head and replied, "N-no, sir."

"Good," Ian said and continued, "Now we're going for a little ride and I'm the navigator."

Behind Ian, Chalmers, Chad and Nancy sat with their backs to the van's side walls.

—

Mary Dinosa was not a happy camper. She was driving an empty school bus on a winding road and following another bus driven by her old partner on the SFPD force, Dwight MacArthur. When Mack pulled off into a turnout and parked she pulled up behind him. Trailing them was the operation command and communications van driven by Snoopy.

When they were all parked, Mack and Dinosa joined Snoopy in her van. When they were settled, Dinosa grumbled, "I never pictured myself as a school bus driver."

—

Jesse, Grant, Chad and Grub arrived at the tree line above the cliff overlooking the compound two hundred feet below. Grub was gasping to catch his breath and rasped, "God, I've got to start working out more."

His companions were busy retrieving and donning their rappelling gear as Grub set up his electronic gear and placed a dish antenna in the crook of a pine tree. He turned on his frequency scanner and plugged in the antenna cable and then connected his lap top. He looped an ear phone on and said, "Grub to Snoopy."

A moment later he heard, "Snoopy back."

"Standby for video feed," Grub said.

Their conversation was being heard by the rest of the team members who now wore ear phones and transmitters on the same frequency.

Grub adjusted some dials on his scanner and then entered data into his lap top and said, "Holy Cow, I've picked up sixteen cameras! You should be receiving video now."

Snoopy, sitting in front of four monitors, acknowledged she had his video feed. Each monitor was split into quadrants representing the video from all sixteen cameras.

A knock on the rear door of the van got everyone's attention.

"It's Ian."

Mack opened the door and gave Ian a hand up into the crowded van. He crouched behind Snoopy and simply said, "Excellent," followed by, "Grub, this is Ian. We're going to need a few minutes here, so you guys standby."

He studied the video from each camera, occasionally asking Snoopy to enlarge a particular quadrant to full screen and to zoom in on certain areas. The first scene on Monitor One showed a foyer area and an armed guard stationed at the entrance. Three tunnels branched off from the otherwise empty foyer. The next scene was a view of a large cavern with a crowd of women, some holding babies, and older children sitting in rows of pews. Their attention was directed at an elderly woman who was standing on a raised platform at the front of the room addressing the others. Ian wished the broadcast included audio. Behind her a tunnel disappeared into darkness. The third quadrant showed a different view of the same grotto from the front of the room. The back of the elderly woman could be seen and the faces of the congregation members. Two armed young men stood guard at the entrance.

The final quadrant of Monitor One was a view of a smaller grotto that showed a man sitting in front of a bank of monitors who was observing the same scenes as the team in the van. The man wore a headset with attached microphone and what appeared to be a two-way radio set off to the side.

Ian pointed and commented, "This must be their communication center."

A rectangular table sat in the middle of the room surrounded by eight chairs. On the far side was a line of a dozen or so bunk beds. Several men were sitting up and appeared to be in conversation. The remaining bunks were occupied by men sleeping.

The final scene of Monitor One was a large warehouse cavern that was stacked with crates of ammunition and fire arms with various stenciled labels designating their contents. The arsenal contained small automatic firearms to fifty caliper machine guns and rifle propelled grenades to shoulder held surface to air missiles. Other crates were labeled C-4 and dynamite explosive and others marked hazardous material. It was obvious to even the casual observer the GWN was armed for a small war.

The remaining three monitors were various views of the compound outside. One view showed the front of the cave's three entrances. Another showed the well-lighted courtyard area and front of the house. A view of another showed the three vents located on top of the cliff. Views of the perimeter including one of the front gate and the two bunkers filled the quadrants of the other monitors. Occasionally a guard would appear walking the perimeter.

"I take it your taping these images," Ian directed his question to Snoopy.

After an affirmative nod, Ian continued, "Okay, begin broadcasting the loop on the camera looking at the air vents now. When I give you the signal, broadcast the video loop on monitors two through four and maintain a live feed on Monitor One. You got that?"

"Yep," Snoopy replied and hitting a key on her console the air vent image blinked.

"Jesse, you and your team can attach the canisters and begin your descent. From what we've seen there are three guards patrolling the east and the west perimeter, but there could be more. Grub, standby and activate the valve releases with your remote upon my signal. Unless it's absolutely necessary, no one fires until my command," Ian said and added, "This operation needs to go down quick and timing is everything and so far the stars are aligned in our favor."

Upon receiving confirmation from everyone, Ian patted Snoopy on the back, kissed Mary and left the van. As he walked toward the Johnson's van, two County Fire and Rescue ambulances pulled into the turn out. Mack walked over and talked to the occupants.

Ian entered Johnson's van and said. "Okay, Claudie old boy, take us to your leader."

As the van approached the compound's gate, Ian said, "Okay Grub, open the valves. Snoopy, keep us advised of what's happening in the caves. Jesse, are you guys in position?"

"That's affirmative," Jesse replied.

A man dressed in camo fatigues and carrying a rifle emerged from a bunker on the left of the gate as the van pulled up. Ian, sitting behind the driver's seat pushed the muzzle of his hand gun with enough force that Claude could feel its pressure in the middle of his back and said, "If you want to survive this, I hope you don't forget your lines."

He ducked under a tarp that covered the van's cargo area.

The man in the fatigues approached the van and said, "Claude, what are you doing here?"

Attempting to sound convincing, Claude replied, "Joshua instructed me to deliver this shipment as soon as it came in. He said it was very important."

"Joshua ain't here. Let me check with Abraham," he said turning his head and saying something into a two way radio.

A moment later the man turned around and said, "Abe said to proceed and he'll meet you in front of the house."

The gate swung open and Claude pulled the van forward. It disappeared over a rise and Ian said, "Slow down Claude," and then added, "Go you guys and God speed."

The rear doors of the van swung open and Chad and Nancy jumped out, tumbling to break their falls. Getting to their feet they raced in opposite directions until they reached the tree line on either side of the road and proceeded back towards the bunkers.

An elderly man with a long gray beard and dressed in overalls was coming down the steps from the porch of the house when the van pulled up. He walked to the driver's side and upon arriving, said, "Claude, Joshua didn't say anything about a special delivery..."

From behind, Claude heard a muffled pop and a red hole appeared in the center of Abe's brow before he crumpled to the ground.

"What the...?" Claude started before he felt a hand cover his mouth and a sharp pain in his neck. His eyes rolled up before he slumped in his seat passed out.

Mack and Dinosa were gathered around Snoopy watching Monitor One in the back of the command center van. The children were acting up and the women were swaying around seemingly performing something like the dance of the Seven Veils. In another quadrant the men appeared to be singing until fights started breaking out. Within a minute or two the scenes looked like they were in slow motion. One by one people started laying or falling down.

Snoopy reported these actions to the rest of the team and Ian then said, "Okay everybody, fire when ready."

From all sides of the compound pops could be heard and an occasional rifle retort. The team members were all armed with AR16 automatic rifles with attached fire and sound suppressors along with 9 mm side arms with similar muzzle attachments.

Chalmers ran to the rear door of the home and Ian ascended the front steps and stood with his back to the wall next to the front door with his pistol raised, the barrel resting on his temple. A moment later the door flew open and two armed men ran out. Ian shot the second man in the back of the head and when the leading man turned he shot him in the temple. They both dropped immediately. Ian checked their pulses and confirming they were dead returned to the door and said, "Chuck, what's happening there?"

Chalmers replied, "No signs of movement here."

"Okay, let's enter," Ian said.

Entering the front room Ian observed four elderly women on their knees praying, "Yea, though I walk through the shadows of the valley or death I shall fear…"

Chalmers appeared through a hall at the opposite side of the room and said, "Ah, Jesus."

One by one they anesthetized each of the women and then proceeded to clear the rest of the house. Finding it empty, Ian said, "Nancy, Chad, report."

Nancy came back, "Front gate neutralized."

"Jesse, what's up?" Ian asked.

Jesse came back, "Perimeter secured."

"Okay, bring up the ambulances and the busses. Nancy and Chad, you can hitch a ride. Everybody else, let's rendezvous in the courtyard."

Grub sat high above the cliff in the tree line observing everything unfolding below through night vision glasses and couldn't help himself from commenting, "Wow, you guys are amazing. It was well worth the price of admission."

"Grub, I almost forgot about you. How are you doing?" Ian said.

"I'm freezing my balls off, but it was worth it," Grub came back.

"Well, pack it up and make your way back to the snow tractor. Remove the canisters and make sure you leave the transmitter. We'll see you back at the house," Ian said looking at Chalmers and smiling.

The ambulances, busses and communication van pulled into the courtyard and parked. Nancy, Chad and Snoopy exited the van, each toting a large box containing gas masks. Mack and Dinosa climbed out of their busses and Mack and Snoopy walked over to meet the EMTs gathered outside one of the ambulances.

The team rendezvoused in front of the house where each gathered a gas mask.

"Let's make this quick and clean," Ian said.

Each team member donned gas masks and the group moved toward the cave entrances. Chalmers opened the door to the first cave and he, Chad and Nancy entered the foyer area. A young man dressed in fatigues lay sprawled on the floor just inside the room. Chalmers bent down, rolled the man over and shackled and cuffed him. He then entered the first of three tunnels that branched off from the foyer. Chad and Nancy entered the other two.

He was amazed to find himself inside a sophisticated, underground residential apartment complex with doors leading off the tunnel hallway to primitive living quarters. He entered and cleared each apartment, finding all of them vacant.

Ian led the rest of the team into the second cave where they discovered two armed men laying passed out close to the entrance of the large grotto. Women and children lay unconscious among the chairs that filled the large grotto known as the community center.

The two men were shackled to each other and cuffed and the team moved through the room to a tunnel in the rear. Dinosa remained behind to guard the room as the rest of the team made their way through the tunnel and emerged at the communication center and barracks area. Fifteen men lay in various positions among the bunks and in front of the work counter that lined one side of the room. Some of the men had bloody noses and split lips, the result of the drunken brawl they had waged earlier.

The unconscious men were dragged and lined up in the middle of the room and cuffed and shackled to each other. Steve remained behind as the team returned to the community center. Some of the women were showing signs of life with quiet moans.

Nancy positioned herself on the raised platform and took off her gas mask and inhaled deeply several times. She stood waiting for a few minutes before saying, "Its' all clear."

The rest of the team removed their masks and from the entrance to the cave, Chalmers turned, waved at Mack and said, "Bring 'em in."

Mack led two EMT teams into the cavern and they began moving about the group of waking women and children conducting preliminary examinations and setting up triage.

On the platform, Nancy spoke through a megaphone in a calm and soothing voice, "Let me assure you all that you will be fine. You were gassed with a nonlethal drug that will leave you temporarily disoriented and most likely with a headache.

"We are not here to harm you. Please do as you are told and I promise you, you will be well taken care of."

She repeated this statement as the women and now children began to sober up.

Upon seeing the two shackled men, who had earlier been their guardians, being led out of the room's entrance, the elderly lady who had been addressing the group cried, "Where are the rest of our men?"

"They have been taken prisoners and will be well treated," Nancy replied.

Ian and Chambers wandered outside to a light snow fall. Chambers squinted and looked up to the heavens and signed, "Jesus, Ian, is it over?"

Ian took a deep breath and replied, "Maybe this chapter, but I fear the book is not."

A dark sedan pulled up and parked behind the ambulances followed by a grey bus marked 'Federal Convict Transport'. Two men in suits got out of the sedan and three uniformed men carrying riot shot guns emerged from the bus.

The two men in suits approached Ian and Chambers and the shorter one carrying a brief case asked, "Is U.S. Justice Department Special Investigator Mary Dinosa here?"

From behind them, escorting two shackled men, Dinosa yelled, "I'm Dinosa. Who are you?"

"I'm Agent Faulk with the U.S. Marshall's Service and this is Agent Sauer. We have about thirty John Doe arrest warrants and we've been instructed to take custody of the prisoners from you," the shorter man said handing her a piece of paper.

Dinosa looked at the paper and saw it was a Justice Department application for arrest warrants. Scanning the page she realized it was for the arrest of those responsible for the Synagogue bombing in San Francisco and was submitted by Justice Department Prosecutor Valerie Kane.

"Excellent," she simply replied.

—

It was 10:15 pm in San Francisco, California. Valerie Kane sat at her desk in her seventh story office of the Federal Building, accompanied by her assistant, Gloria Darden and sometimes partner of Mary Dinosa, and Inspector Kyle Montgomery.

They were engaged in nervous idle chat when the phone on her desk rang. The sound temporarily startled everyone. Trying to steady her trembling hand, Kane picked up.

"Hello, Valerie Kane here."

With a stoic face, she listened to the voice on the other end and after what seemed to Gloria and Kyle as hours, she simply said, "Thank you," and hung up the phone.

Maintaining her sober expression she looked across at her two comrades and said, "That was Agent Faulk with the Marshall's Service," and then breaking into a broad smile she added, "Eighteen arrest warrants were served a half hour ago on members of the Great White Nation. They are in the Marshall's custody and being transported to the maximum security federal prison outside Elko, Nevada. I've been told, with the exception of several resisters, the subjects surrendered peacefully."

A collective sigh went up and Kane scurried around from behind her desk to a group hug and jumping like teammates who'd just won the World Series.

As the jubilation subsided, Kyle asked, "How is Dinosa?"

Bending down in front of a filing cabinet and opening the large bottom drawer, Kane said, "Except for a few bangs and bruises, she's fine."

She withdrew a bottle of Makers Mark bourbon and three cocktail glasses from the drawer and placed them on her desk. She poured and half-filled the glasses and then as an afterthought, she topped the three glasses off and handed one to each of her friends.

Raising her glass, Valerie said, "Here's to Bernie Rusk, Mary Dinosa and 'who were those masked men'?"

—

The corporate Cessna Citation Jet taxied across the tarmac to the private aircraft area at San Francisco International Airport and stopped in front of a hangar identified as 'O'Farrell Enterprises'. A black limousine was parked in front of a dark SUV inside the hangar.

Sheila Lamont, daughter of Sean O'Farrell, emerged from the back seat of the limousine and walked out to greet Corky Burmeister as she ascended the steps from the plane's fuselage.

Corky had tried to make herself presentable before landing, but she still looked haggard.

After they introduced themselves, Sheila said, "You must be exhausted. There's a wet bar in the limo and we'll get you a refreshment. It'll take an hour or so to get home to a soak in the tub, a hot meal and a warm bed. Please accept our hospitality. You probably have a million questions and I'll do my best to answer them."

"Thank you so much, but you're the one that must have a million questions," Corky replied graciously.

"No I don't. You're accepted unconditionally and I hope you can relax."

—

Sol Goldsmith and Grub stood on the porch waiting to greet the team as their vehicles pulled into the farm house driveway and parked in front. Seeing everyone was accounted for, Sol turned and hugged a startled Grub.

Once inside, everyone gathered in the front room and Ian said, "I'd like to congratulate everybody for our successful mission. However, after retrieving their birth logs and comparing that to the dead and the survivors, we've discovered several members are unaccounted for.

"We have reason to believe that their leader, Frank Johnson, who now goes by the name Joshua, and three to four other men, had departed the compound before our arrival. Other documents we recovered from the house indicate these men are undertaking another mission we know only as 'Armageddon Spring'.

"Let's all go home now, but I'm asking you all to remain on standby until we can gain intelligence on their latest mission."

"I only have one question," Snoopy said.

"Go ahead," Ian said.

"Where are the women and children going and what's going to happen to them?" she asked.

Chalmers answered, "They are being bussed to Fairchild Air Force Base outside of Spokane, Washington, and Bernard Rusk has arranged air transportation for them to a compound in New Mexico. That facility was constructed right after World War II to accommodate European Jewish refugees we anticipated would be arriving in the United States. It was never utilized, but the CIA covertly took over control of the facility and has maintained it over the years for situations just like this one.

"They will be evaluated and a course for debriefing and rehabilitation will be determined by the doctors there. I'm told that women and children of these kinds of religious sects have been subjugated and are very pliable and positive results are the usual outcome. Some of the older boys will be more difficult and in some cases it will take longer."

—

CHAPTER FOURTEEN

"So, I take it we haven't found Corky yet," the President said setting across from Santiago in the Oval Office.

"Not yet, but we have determined she was picked up by local police and taken to their station soon after Al Long reported in. We believe she met a man there and the last known sighting was her getting into a car with him. We assume this man works for Rusk. From there the trail goes cold, but we have issued an APB to all police agencies in the D.C. area and we're monitoring all airports, train stations and bus depots. I'm confident we'll find her soon," Santiago reported.

"What's our cover plan?" the President asked, caressing his chin.

"Tomorrow we'll publicly announce her resignation due to physical and mental exhaustion. We're hoping your announcement later this evening surrounding, what we're now calling operation 'Justice', the successful attack and elimination of the GWN will certainly trump the news of her resignation.

"We've already prepared a simple press release we'll issue announcing her resignation and expressing your deep regrets and appreciation for her dedicated service."

President Benjamin lowered and rubbed his head and groaned, "Jesus, this could get ugly."

"Mister President, please put your mind at ease. We will find Miss Burmeister and deal with her, and after tonight, believe me, you will be hailed as a national hero and savior," Santiago cajoled and added, "It's time we meet everyone in the Situation Room, sir."

The two departed the oval office and proceeded down the hall to the elevator, escorted by two Secret Service Agents. They entered and descended one hundred feet below the White House. When they exited they were met by a group of Secret Service Agents in full body armor and armed with automatic weapons who guarded the foyer area and the halls leading away in three directions.

They proceeded down the hall in front of them to a door at the end where Santiago swiped his access card and opened the door. He allowed the President entry and followed him into the well-lighted room. The men and women in the room all stood as he strolled in and he immediately said, "Please, as you were and continue your work."

One wall of the room was lined with computer stations and manned by civilians. In the center of the room sat a large oblong table surrounded by twelve unoccupied chairs. Several men in military dress along with the Director of Homeland Security and two of his assistants were crowded around a large screen television sitting in leather cushioned chairs in the far corner of the room. The official White House photographer was moving about the room taking pictures to document this historical event.

Room was made and two more chairs were wheeled to the front of the television. The President acknowledged the Homeland Security Deputy and the Generals and Admiral that stood to greet him.

Taking a seat, the president said, "Please, gentlemen, be seated and Charlie, tell me what's happening."

"Well, Mister President, it's about 4:30 pm their time and dark. The four drones are approaching the target. They are being escorted and supported by two Cherokee attack helicopters. Our FBI and ATF agents are standing by at a safe distance from the target and they've evacuated civilians from nearby homes.

"Our drones are each armed with two bunker busting missiles and the choppers are armed with fifty caliper mounted machine guns with armor piercing ammunition. The drones have tagged the targets and ready. We're just awaiting your command, sir."

Realizing his next words would be etched in the annuls of history and chronicled around the world, the President cleared his throat and solemnly said, "May God bless these brave women and men, and may God bless the United States, fire at will!"

Santiago remained stoic but was thinking, the 'God' word will probably alienate some of his supporters, but putting the women before the men was a pure stroke of genius.

The scene on the television set before them, as seen through night vision lenses, showed the entire compound. A gate blocked the entrance road and was guarded by armed men in bunkers on either side of the road. The road led to a house and a barn that sat before a looming granite cliff.

Suddenly and almost simultaneously the house and the barn exploded in clouds of smoke and fire followed by a succession of tremendous explosions emanating from the cliff behind them. The face of the cliff started to slowly descend in an avalanche of rocks and boulders and disappeared behind a billowing cloud of dust.

Martha was in the kitchen of their Squaw Mountain cabin peeling potatoes and her husband Will was slouched in his easy chair in front of the television in the living room snoring peacefully when the house began to shake. The shaking was followed by a thunderous roar that echoed off the canyon walls.

Awakened, Will leapt from his chair and ignoring the sharp pain in his back, yelled, "Martha, are you all right?"

The house was still trembling and the roar still echoed as Martha appeared in the doorway of the front room holding a paring knife in one hand and a half naked potato in the other.

Wide eyed she mumbled, "What the hell was that?"

In the White House Situation Room everyone's eyes were glued to the scene developing on the television in silence.

One of the General's broke the silence, remarking, "Holy Shit! Those were secondary explosions. They must have had a shit load of explosives stashed in their arsenal."

The President rose from his seat and simply said, "Charlie keep me posted and I'll need a preliminary report within the hour."

He instructed Santiago to remain and he left the room.

—

The black Humvee, towing a small canopied trailer, turned right off of Highway 57 and passed under an archway that read, 'Heaven's Gate Private Community', and pulled up to a security kiosk and gate that block their way. An armed guard wearing a heavy parka, ear muffs and wool gloves stepped out of the kiosk and approached the driver's side window.

"May I ask you what your business is here, sir?" the man asked.

"My name is Joshua Johnson and we're here to visit Bud Blackwell. He's expecting us."

"Yes sir, he is," the guard said and continued, "Just continue down this road to the end and turn right. His house is sits right above the river."

"Thank you, son," Joshua replied.

The road wound gently down a slope. The sun was now up above the mountain horizon and revealed a landscape of rolling hills that descended to the river below. A variety of leafless birch, giant red fir and cedar, and lodge pole pine trees crowded together between open snow covered fields. Occasionally a graveled driveway off the main road would lead to sometimes a simple cabin and other times to affluent estate homes. All of the homes appeared to be recently constructed.

As they approached the river the road ended at a tee. Joshua turned right and drove until the levy road terminated at a large two story cedar sided home. A large man with a bushy brown mustache wearing a wool coat and knitted cap descended the porch stairs and walked to the Humvee.

Joshua exited his vehicle and met the man with his hand outstretched.

"You must be Bud Blackwell," he said amiably.

"And you must be Joshua Johnson. Welcome to Heaven's Gate," Bud replied.

"Glad to be here and it sure is aptly named. This truly is God's country."

"I'd invite you in, but the family's just rising and really not prepared to meet visitors," Bud said handing Joshua a key.

"That's totally understandable. We have arrived a little early."

Before releasing his grip on the key, Blackwell's face turned grim and he said, "You're welcome here as long as you know and obey the rules. We won't tolerate any trouble making."

Johnson smiled broadly and said, "Me and the boys know your rules and have no fear, we mean no harm and you can expect no trouble from us."

Blackburn returned the smile and said, "Okay then. You're place is the log cabin just down the road you come in on. Just continue past the tee and you'll run smack into it. I'll be along a little later and we can chat."

—

"Okay everybody, let's go over the rules," Tom Featherstone, the interim Presidential Press Secretary started, standing in front of a podium with the Presidential Seal attached and located in the center of the stage in the White House Press room.

Checking his wrist watch, he continued, "In about two minutes President Benjamin will be out to make an announcement. He will speak briefly about the facts and outcome of last evening's events in north Idaho. We've allowed only one video camera in the room, but you all have access to the feed, so I would take this opportunity the ensure that your networks are connected.

"The President will not be taking any questions at this time. You will be given a press release folder containing a more detailed account of the raid with pictures and video clips immediately following his announcement."

A few minutes later the room fell silent as the President approached the podium and looked grimly into the camera with the teleprompter set to one side.

"Good morning ladies and gentlemen and fellow citizens. This morning I can tell you the threat of the Great White Nation, who has brought terror and destruction of unequaled proportion from coast to coast in our great nation, is over."

This announcement was met with a round of applause from those in attendance.

The President continued, "Because of the actions and intelligence gathering of many great and heroic men and women of our Homeland Security Office, the FBI and the ATF, last night I gave the order to attack the compound and headquarters of the Great White Nation which was located in northern Idaho.

"I took the extreme measure of using armed drones in the attack and I will live with any consequences that action may bring. I ordered this tactic after being advised that these terrorists were well armed and prepared to repel a ground attack and that such an attack would certainly result in many casualties on our side.

"I'm happy to report that there were zero casualties to any of our people conducting the operation or innocent citizens. I can tell you these terrorists were a relatively small group of male dissidents of a fanatical religious white superiority sect. The remains of fourteen well-armed and equipped men were discovered in the compound and, I'm told, that includes their leader.

"Homeland Security and the FBI have an ongoing investigation as to their identities and origins. I am confident their joint investigation will reveal all of the facts surrounding this group and we will act on that report and their conclusions so that acts similar to those perpetrated by these hate mongers will never happen again."

He paused and his lips tightened before he continued, "I made a promise to you who elected me to be your President, that we would be the most transparent administration in our Nation's history and I believe we've lived up to that. I stated earlier that I will live with the consequences of my decisions and I welcome the critics of my actions."

He raised his chin and his volume, "I am proud to say, because of my actions and those of my fellow Americans, we have eliminated this threat to our nation's safety and sovereignty. May God bless you all and may God bless the United States of America."

He turned and started to walk briskly off the stage. Questions were being directed at him by inquiring reporters from all corners of the room when above them all, the shrilled yell of a woman reporter from the back of the room could be clearly heard by all.

"Can you tell us anything about where Cory Burmeiser might be?"

Upon hearing this, the President stutter stepped, but without acknowledging the question he resumed his stride and continued to walk off the stage.

—

Chalmers pulled into his driveway. Christmas lights lined the eaves of his home and his front door and porch. A miniature nativity scene was up and lighted in the corner of the yard.

"Ah crap," he said with a feeling of guilt. This was the first time he had missed the family pre-Christmas ritual of decorating the house.

After parking, he grabbed his bag from the back seat and took the stairs two at a time to the back door. Opening the door and entering the kitchen he found his wife with her back to him in front of the stove.

She whirled around and said, "Oh, you startled me!"

Wiping her hands on her apron she ran to Chalmers and yelled out, "Jennifer, your Dad's home!"

Chalmers dropped his bag and they hugged. Jennifer ran into the room and squealed, "Oh Pop, you made it home for Christmas."

They group hugged and then Colleen said, "Why don't you help your father unpack so I can prepare supper."

Jennifer followed her father out of the kitchen, down the hall and into the master bedroom where Chalmers threw his bag on the bed.

"Can you tell me where you've been?" she asked.

"I can tell you I've been in Idaho and its beautiful there. You'd love it. We should plan a family trip there sometime. I'm told there's some great ski resorts in the area."

"Did you catch the bad guys?" she asked feigning innocence.

"Yes we did," Chalmers answered, starting to feel uncomfortable.

"We watched the President on television this morning saying that they had killed the people responsible for the Synagogue bombing and the other terrorist attacks. Did you participate in that?"

"No," Chalmers replied and trying to change the subject asked, "Would you mind bringing in the dirty clothes hamper from the bathroom?"

After unpacking, Chalmers draped his arm over his daughter's shoulder and they walked out of the bedroom, down the hall and into the living room. A decorated Christmas tree sat in the far corner next to the front bay window.

Colleen was sitting in the loveseat and Chalmers sat down beside her and laid his arm across the back of her neck. Jennifer took a seat across from them.

"I'm really sorry I wasn't here to help put up the decorations," Chalmers said and added. "I hope you got our neighbor Barney to help."

"Geez Pop, like Mom and I can't set up and move a ladder and climb up and down it? We are hopelessly frail and useless without the help of a man. It took all of our strength to drag the crates out of the garage and struggled to set up the little baby Jesus scene. I thought Mom was going to pass out," Jennifer groaned sarcastically.

"Your apology is accepted," Colleen said sympathetically and smiling.

"So, the smells coming from the kitchen tells me we're going to have a sumptuous dinner tonight," Chalmers said, again trying to change the subject.

"Mom banned me from the house tonight so I've made plans to go to the movies with Matt. She says she wants you all to herself tonight," Jennifer said indignantly.

"I did no such thing…" Colleen started defensively when a knock on the front door mercifully interrupted her.

Jennifer opened the door to Matthew O'Farrell who stepped in and mannerly said, "Good evening, Mister and Misses Chalmers."

Jennifer grabbed a sweater off the back of a chair and Matt by the arm said, "Come on, let's get out of here before the old witch decides to boil us for the supper."

Before Colleen could protest they were gone. She turned and kissed her husband and said, "Actually, I did suggest it would be nice if you and I could be alone tonight. I have a special candle lit dinner planned and the hot tub is on and heating and the wine is in the ice bucket."

—

Mary Dinosa lay soaking in a bubble bath tub and closed her eyes, relaxed for the first time in days and allowed the warmth of the moment to ease her aching body.

She whispered out loud, "Man, I got to give this shit up"

Her mind wondered back to her days on the SFPD and her first day after being assigned to Homicide Detail and being partnered with the gruff old Senior Inspector Chalmers. It was the first time since graduating from the Police Academy that she felt intimidated and it didn't help when he began their relationship by saying, "Okay rookie, just keep your mouth shut and learn and you'll be fine."

If anybody else had confronted her in a like manner, she would have promptly kicked their ass. To the surprise of everyone in the department she deferred to her senior officer and the partnership evolved into a match of almost legendary proportions.

A mutual respect developed and Mary found herself falling in love with him. She logically realized how ridiculous her feelings were. He was a happily married family man and could be her father, for Christ's sake. Still she foolishly fantasized about being with him, knowing full well that would never happen.

Then she met Ian O'Farrell and her childish crush on Charles Chalmers began to turn into more like a daughter's love and affection. Her first impression of Ian was not a good one. She thought him brash and arrogant and he reminded her of all the super macho types she had dated through the years. He was certainly brave and she began to admire his benevolent yet effective leadership qualities.

Her opinion completed the U-turn when she witnessed his honest and heartfelt feelings for his fellow comrades in arms when they spread one of their friend's ashes at sea. In the months that followed she looked for signs from him that would signal a mutual feeling.

Oddly, but ironically appropriate, that moment came on the eighteenth green of a Phoenix golf course when she slapped handcuffs on an international arms and drug dealer and glanced at Ian and recognized the sparkle in his eyes. The spark turned into a raging inferno that night when they consumed each other in this very apartment.

Her thoughts were interrupted when she heard the gate of the cargo elevator open and a familiar voice yell out, "It's just me!"

"I'm in here," Dinosa returned a yell.

Ian entered the front room carrying a bag and paused to retrieve a TV tray from its' rack before entering the bathroom.

"We have to do something about the security for this place. I'll send some people over tomorrow," he said as he set up the tray and sat down on the floor facing her.

"Anything you say, your Highness," Dinosa replied smiling sarcastically.

Ian pulled several boxes of Japanese food from the take out bag and positioned them on the tray and then stripped the paper off a set of chopsticks. Plucking a piece of gioza, he dunked it in a mustard soy sauce and using his other hand as a drip guard he moved the morsel toward her mouth.

She opened her mouth and sucked the morsel in, mumbling almost inaudibly, "Mmm, I feel like a queen."

"This reminds me of when I was a kid. Every Mother's Day, my brothers and sisters and I would prepare breakfast and serve our mother in bed," Ian said.

"So, you're telling me, feeding me Japanese take out while I'm laying naked in a bubble bath, reminds you of serving your mother breakfast in bed on Mother's Day. Oh Ian, you're such a romantic."

—

The morning sun shone bright in the eastern skies as Chalmers stopped in front of Sol Goldsmith's Sean Cliff Avenue home. Sol scurried from his front porch and trotted out to Chalmers' car and jumped in the passenger seat.

"Morning Sol, did ya get a good nights' sleep?"

"Yep and I feel like a spring chicken, how 'bout you?"

"Can't say I got a lot of sleep, but I'm feeling refreshed," Chalmers winked.

As they crested the hill on the Pacific Coast Highway above Park Presidio, the towers of the Golden Gate Bridge rose in front of them through the coastal fog below and looked like tines of a trident emerging from the smoke of hell.

"Do you have any idea what this Spring Armageddon is all about?" Goldsmith asked.

"I don't have a clue, but you can bet your sweet ass we'll find out," Chalmers replied.

"I understand Grub has all the data and intelligence we recovered from the GWN compound and he's feeding it into some kind of a 'probability' program in his computer. He's not real optimistic that it'll produce results, but I'm sure glad he's on our side," Sol commented.

"Amen to that. To be honest with you, I'm barely able to turn a computer on. 'Windows for Dummies' is even beyond my comprehension," Chalmers groaned.

"Don't feel pregnant. I think it has something to do with our generation. We grew up using sticks as guns and playing cowboy and Indians. This generation grew up with digital play stations, blowing up asteroids and traveling through time to zap would be aliens bent on destroying our planet," Sol commiserated.

"You know Sol, what happened at your Synagogue, as an example, makes me wonder what God's plan is for our planet. I mean, just look at the corruption and evil our little 'Justice Foundation' has uncovered. Do you believe evil may eventually win out?" Chalmers pondered.

"That, sir, is the great mystery. Albert Einstein compared good and evil to light and dark. He postulated that dark is nothing more than the absence of light and life cannot be sustained without light. If light ceases to exist so does life as we understand it. In turn, he believed evil is the absence of good and life cannot exist if there is no goodness.

"I don't pretend to know what our Creator's plan is for mankind, but I do believe that as long as there is goodness left in our world, it will survive," Sol said.

The two men drove on in silence, dipping down into the fog and crossing the Golden Gate Bridge. They exited at the Sausalito off ramp and negotiated the switchback road until they turned off onto the driveway that would lead them to the O'Farrell estate.

They were met at the front door of the magnificent manor by Sean O'Farrell who greeted and invited them in and escorted them to the den. Present in the room were George Armstrong, Ian O'Farrell, Bernard Rusk and Corky Burmeister.

After introductions were made, Rusk said, "I've invited Miss Burmeister here to enlighten us on some of her White House experiences and what happened to her a couple of nights ago."

He nodded at Corky who remained seated. Chalmers noticed, although she appeared nervous and slightly ruffled, she was an attractive black woman with a short, shaggy haircut and appeared to be in her early thirties. She certainly didn't look like the tall, confident, self-assured woman he had seen many times standing in front of veteran reporters, answering and deflecting tough questions in the White House Press Room with cameras rolling.

She started with her account of how she had met the charismatic leader some twelve years earlier when she was a university student and how taken she was with his caring and self-confident ways. She explained that although at the time he was married with two young daughters, she was naïve enough to be 'sucked' in by his charms and was happy to share stolen moments in bed as his mistress and by his side conducting the

Nation's business. She sensed that his wife was aware of their trysts and chose to ignore them.

She had served the President faithfully and had been at his beckoned call for years. As she witnessed firsthand the corruption build around him and eventually turn this idealistic young man into a hateful opportunist, she began to question her own motivations.

Her mood changed to indignant anger as she began describing the events of a few nights ago and frightened to 'death' by the incident, she decided her only escape was to join the opposition. She finished by expressing her deep appreciation to Mister Rusk and the hospitality of the O'Farrell's.

"Thank you, Miss Burmeister," Rusk said and addressing everyone else, continued, "We've asked Miss Burmeister to document the corruption she witnessed and just touched on. For the record and based on the time I'm told she's spent on her computer in Sean's study since her arrival, she's been very diligent.

"Forgive me Corky, but I'm going to ask you to return now to the study. We have matters to discuss in private," Rusk requested.

After Corky had left the room, Rusk continued, "According to Corky, the President and his men suspect I'm working with a group such as the 'Justice Foundation', but so far they haven't identified you. Until we find and eliminate Frank, aka

Joshua, Johnson and his remaining three or four followers, we intend to maintain your group's anonymity.

"As in any operation, timing is the principal element for success. When the time is right to release the information we have accumulated, it will require sacrifices and undoubtedly one of those sacrifices could be your anonymity. I wanted all of you to know that and I'd like your approval to proceed."

"Bernie," Armstrong began, "We all realized that our anonymity would be jeopardized when we agreed to join you and we discussed the possibility of our anonymity being exposed. We decided that the threat to our country was worth the risk.

"The only thing we ask is, before you release your information, we be advised and that you keep us abreast on how and when you plan to release it. We have all conducted illegal acts and we'll need to protect ourselves."

"I appreciate that, George, and of course that request will be honored," Rusk said.

—

CHAPTER FIFTEEN

The President sat at his desk in his 'Inner Chamber' shifting anxiously in his chair. Paulo Santiago sat across from him equally as nervous. The president laid both of his palms on the desk and leapt up with fire in his eyes.

"God damn it!" he yelled while pounding a fist on the desk top, "Paulo, I've relied on you for years to cover my ass! Now you tell me you've allowed me to stand before my constituents and lie to them?!"

Santiago glanced at the door to make sure it was closed and said, "Don't shoot the messenger, sir."

"You're more than a fucking messenger! I want your letter of resignation on my desk by noon!" the President cried.

Santiago adjusted his tie, jutted his chin and said, "I don't think that would be the right course of action to take at this time. You've already had one high level staff member resign this week. If I resigned, it would send a signal that panic has set in.

"I suggest we let the dust settle and if at that time you still wish for me to resign, I'll gladly do it."

The President sat back down and slumped in his chair. He spent a moment in thought and then said in an eerily calm voice, "Okay, you're right, of course. Tell me the whole story."

"Well, there were a total of eighteen bodies and body parts recovered from the compound and sent to the FBI forensic lab here for autopsy and chemical analyses. The preliminary findings say these men were dead for approximately fifteen to twenty hours before our attack..."

The President interrupted, "You mean to tell me we attacked people who were already dead?"

"It appears someone beat us to the punch," Santiago said attempting to maintain his composure before continuing, "We've suspected for some time that Rusk is working with some unidentified independent and underground group. We believe this group discovered the GWN's location before we did and conducted a raid just hours before our attack."

"Who all knows about the autopsy results?" the President asked.

"The coroner who conducted the autopsies, of course, and probably an assistant or two would be aware of the findings. Then there would be the stenographer who transcribed the report, the Chief FBI Field Agent, his supervisor and the Director of the FBI.

"The Director has assured us that his field agent and his supervisor are trustworthy and the lab people are bound by law not to reveal the results and have been strongly reminded of that fact. We are keeping close eyes on all of them," Santiago reported.

"Our intelligence told us when we found these terrorists we would find a community of people including women and children. Where are they?" the President asked.

"If there were other people at the compound they would have been in cave dwellings at the time of our attack and if so, that will be their eternal tomb. The information we have released to the media makes no mention of any other people or cave dwellings, only that one cave contained the group's arsenal of arms and explosives," Santiago said.

"You mean we buried people a live?" the President said, raising his voice.

"Sir, with all due respect, you knew full well the likelihood that there would be women and children there when you gave the order to fire. They were casualties of war," Santiago replied.

"Shit, shit, shit…who else knows about this possibility," the President moaned, slumping down farther in his chair.

"Only people with equal culpability, sir," Santiago smirked.

"Okay," the President sighed, "Where are we at locating Miss Burmeister?"

"Our best people are on it. We have reason to believe she's sought refuge with family in Florida. We'll find her soon,"

Santiago lied, thinking it best not to burden the President with the fact that he didn't have a clue.

"How about this super-secret group of so called patriots?" the President moaned again.

"Finding them and eliminating them is our top priority. When we do find them, they will be sorry they ever raised a finger to defy us," Santiago stated boldly.

The President covered his face with both hands and with a flick of his fingers indicated Paulo should leave.

Santiago rose and slowly strolled to the door and closed it softly behind him, concerned with his boss' frame of mind.

—

"Merry Christmas everybody! Ho,Ho,Ho!" Steve Cromwell hollered dressed in a Santa Claus suit and appearing to have consumed close to his limit of eggnog. One arm was draped around his wife Nancy who was decked out in an elf's outfit.

Their life sized image appeared on the large screen television that sat centered on the stage in the ballroom of the Armstrong mansion. The couple was standing in front of a video camera located inside the Arrow Head Saloon at their ski lodge in northern California. They were surrounded by fellow revelers and skiers.

The scene they were viewing on their television was members of the team along with their families. Ian and Mary stood arm in arm in the center of the group and above the din in the room, Ian yelled back, "And Merry Christmas to you guys too. Wish you were here!"

"When will we see you guys again?" Nancy hollered.

"Soon, I'm sure," Ian replied.

An obviously inebriated young blond appeared on camera in the lodge and throwing her arms around Steve she planted a kiss on his lips saying, "M-mery Grismas."

The crowd in the ballroom roared with laughter as they watched Steve take an awkward step back, his face flushed.

"You better keep an eye on that hunk of a husband you got there!" Dinosa laughed.

"No fear here, right now his pecker is about as soft as that eggnog he's been consuming!" Nancy exclaimed and then added, "You guys have a great time and we miss you!"

That concluded the simulcast and the group in the ballroom dispersed and wandered back to their tables. Chalmers and Colleen shared a table with Dinosa and Ian and sat across from them. The adjoining table was occupied by the teenagers, Jennifer and Matt, and his sister Shannon and her boyfriend Jeremy Colby.

An old Beatles number was blaring from the stereo and Dinosa stood up and grabbed Chalmers arm saying, "Come on, let's do it."

"Do what?" Chalmers answered knowing what she meant.

"I don't know what you call it, but most of us call it dance," Dinosa retorted.

"You know I can't dance," Chalmers protested.

"Oh, go ahead, you old fart," Colleen urged.

He reluctantly stood up and allowed Dinosa to drag him out onto the dance floor where he awkwardly started flailing his arms and bobbing his head.

"You go, Charles!" Jesse yelled out from his table and followed it with a whistle.

"Get down!" Grant encouraged.

When the song mercifully ended, Chalmers escorted Mary back to their table and before sitting down, Jennifer leaned over from the adjacent table and giggled, "Pop, you looked like a monkey trying to screw a football."

"What did you say…?" and he stopped himself in mid-sentence to the laughter coming from everyone that had heard his daughter.

When the laughter subsided he looked at Colleen and said, "I swear, somehow our daughter is related to Dinosa."

The group laughed even louder.

"I hate to break up this jolly group, but Chuck and Ian, do you think you could break yourselves away for just a moment?" It was George Armstrong asking politely.

"No problem, George," Ian replied.

He and Chalmers followed Armstrong out of the room and to his den. Sean and Sol were already there sitting in easy chairs smoking cigars. George offered a cigar to the two and they both declined.

"I'm sorry to interrupt your fun, but we decided this was a good time to discuss the status of our mission," Armstrong started and continued, "We all know it won't be completed until we eliminate the GWN and expose the President and his men."

"I think we can presume that this 'Armageddon Spring' operation they're planning is set for some time this spring. That gives us at a minimum a little less than three months to find these assholes and eliminate them," Sol said.

"This Johnson fellow has been able to keep an entire community off the radar for over forty years, so he knows what he's doing and going underground with just three or four others shouldn't be that difficult for him," Sean added and continued, "Grub and Snoopy are working on possibilities of where they may be hiding out but success looks grim. We believe determining where there target is and when they plan to execute it are our best chances of stopping it and them. Grub has all the intelligence we recovered and is analyzing it."

"What about Miss Burmeister?" Chalmers asked, "Do we have any leads on the son of a bitch that tried to kill her?"

"Corky says that she recognized him as a man she once saw talking with Paulo Santiago at a D.C. Starbucks some time ago. Bernie Rusk is gathering photographs of any potential suspects and is sending them for Corky to review. We'll deal with this pecker head when he's identified," Armstrong said.

"Jesus," Ian said, slapping his palm to his forehead, "Find a photograph of Alvin Long. He served with the Army Rangers, Delta Force in the nineties. He's the son of a bitch that was tailing Dinosa. I should have thought of him immediately."

"Okay," he continued, "If there's no further questions, let's go enjoy the party and the holiday with our families. Everybody remain on standby and in the meantime, be prepared to roll up your sleeves and get to work when the New Year arrives."

—

Dinosa strolled down the hall until she came to the door marked 'Valerie Kane, Special U.S. Prosecutor, Thirteenth U.S. Judicial District', knocked and opened it.

Kane looked up from behind her desk and rising she exclaimed, "Mary, welcome back stranger. It's so good to see you!"

They met in the middle of the room and hugged.

"It's Christmas Eve, for Christ sake! What the hell are you doing here?" Dinosa asked.

"I could ask you the same question."

"I guess I figured I'd find you here. How're the scum bag prosecutions going?" Dinosa replied.

"You probably haven't heard yet, but Whitehead got shivved today and is lying on a slab at the Coroner's Office. It happened in the cafeteria while he was under federal lock up at San Quentin. Of course there's no suspect," Kane said with a sigh as she turned around and retrieved the bottle of bourbon and two glasses from the lower drawer of a filing cabinet.

"What's that going to do to the investigations and prosecutions?"

"Have a seat, Mary," Valerie said, pouring two stiff portions of bourbon. "It means we'll have to drop the Rico charges on everybody. Whitehead was the only one that could tie everybody to an ongoing criminal activity conspiracy.

"The bright side is, we've forced three Congressmen, a Senator and many on their staffs to resign. They and the other corrupt government officials will probably cop a plea to lesser charges and receive sentences ranging from five to ten years to be served in a federal country club somewhere. I'm preparing plea agreements now."

"Well," Dinosa said, raising her glass," Here's to a Merry fucking Christmas."

"Mary, there's something I need to tell you," Valerie said, after taking a gulp of the whiskey.

"Bernie wants me to be the lead prosecutor after he releases all the shit he has on the President and his Chief of Staff. I've already told him I want out."

"What!?"

"I'm burned out, Mary. As soon as I'm finished with this crap," she said, pointing at the stack of folders on her desk, "I'm going to announce my resignation and take a long vacation.

"I might as well tell you, Nancy and I are getting married. When we get back from our honeymoon, I'm going to throw my hat in the political ring and run for San Francisco District Attorney."

Dinosa sat stunned and silent with her mouth agape. Finally she managed to say, "Holy shit, Valerie! I mean congratulations on your upcoming wedding. Nancy is a fine woman and I'm sure you'll be happy, but do you think changing hats to be the District Attorney will be less stressful than what you're doing now?"

"It's not the work load that stresses me, it's the travel that keeps me away from the one I love. If I win the election, at least it will keep me closer to home," Kane explained.

Dinosa shook her head and sighed, "Valerie, you know I'll support any decision you make."

"Thank you, Mary, and that brings me to another question. If I am elected, would you consider coming on board as my Chief Investigator?" Kane asked.

"That's a trip I wouldn't miss," Dinosa said and added as an afterthought, "At least you'll get the gay and lesbian vote."

—

CHAPTER SIXTEEN

"Hah, hah, hah!" Al Long roared. "This just keeps on getting better. You and the President ordered the killing of a bunch of dead people?"

Paulo Santiago, disguised wearing a fake beard and Redskin ball cap, glanced around the bar to see if Long's outburst had garnered any attention and was relieved to see the only other customers in the dive were busy with their own conversations or too drunk to pay attention to anyone.

"This is serious, Al. Someone pulled off a military style attack just before we got there. Do you have any idea who might have done this?" Santiago whispered desperately.

Long thought for a moment and remembered being made while tailing Mary Dinosa. It was more than a coincidence. He chuckled, "I know exactly who did this, but that information is going to cost you a bundle."

"How much, and how much to eliminate the problem?"

"Two hundred thousand for the information, up front, and two million, half now and the balance upon completion, for eliminating your problem," Long said with a sinister smile.

"Geez, that's quite a bit more than your going rate," Santiago whined.

"You don't know who you're up against," Long snapped.

"Alright, give me a minute," Santiago replied.

He rose from the table and walked out of the bar into the cool misty night and dialed a number on his cell phone. A minute later he returned to the table in the seedy bar.

"It'll take about ten minutes to transfer the money to your account," he said.

Long produced a smart phone from his coat pocket and dialed a number and sat it on the table. A few minutes later the phone beeped and he looked at the display. It indicated seven hundred thousand dollars had been deposited to his account.

"Excellent," he remarked, and looking up at Santiago said, "While I was tailing Mary Dinosa, I told you I'd been made by her date. Well, her boyfriend is Ian O'Farrell. He's a former Navy Seal Commander that I met on a black op mission. He and along with some of his friends are among the few people who could have pulled this off.

"His connection with Miss Dinosa is more than a coincidence."

"I'll get you a dossier on Ian O'Farrell. This has to be done quickly," Santiago remarked.

Taking his leave, Long said, "I'll be in touch."

—

"We mourn the loss of our family members, for we are all sons and daughters of God. And God so loved the world he gave up his only begotten son. And after three days, Jesus rose from the dead to sit at his Father's side in heaven," Joshua Johnson preached to his three young followers sitting in the living room of the cabin at 'Heaven's Gate Private Community'.

"Last night I had a vision from God and he was pleased. He told me our family would soon be at his side and he instructed me and us to continue on our mission. We are to mourn for thirty days and thirty nights and then venture on, into the land of Canaan and according to his Will, Armageddon will commence.

"Let us pray…"

—

Santiago beamed with confidence and pride as he strolled into the Oval Office and laid the morning copy of the 'New York Post' newspaper in front of the President. Above the fold on the front page a one inch headline spanned the entire page and read;

PRESIDENTIAL ACTION ELIMINATES GWN THREAT

And underneath the bold headline, two stories appeared under the sub headlines;

Heroic Assault by HLS and FBI Brings End to Domestic Terrorist Sect

And;

Poll Indicates 82% Approval of President's Action

"I'd also, Mister President, direct your attention to the Editorial Page where an op-ed piece submitted by San Francisco Mayor Ed Bradford calls you a great and heroic President and compares you to Abraham Lincoln," Santiago exclaimed.

President Benjamin scanned the articles with amusement and opened the Editorial Section and beamed, "Make sure we send a thank you note to Mayor Bradford."

"Yes, sir," Santiago replied.

Benjamin put the paper aside, looked across the desk at Santiago and said sternly, "Okay, what's our response when Rusk issues a statement that our raid was unnecessary and incompetent?"

"We deny it. We deny everything," Paulo replied and continued, "Sir, we have public opinion on our side. We counter by saying Rusk and his people are desperately attempting to usurp your authority. Actually, if he acts soon, we can use it to our tactical advantage. Right now you are a national hero and your approval rating is at a record high."

"What's the reaction on Capitol Hill?"

"Gabe Stolich in the Senate and John Garcia in the Congress are calling for Senate and Congressional investigations, but after the licking their party took in the last election, there's little support from many of their colleagues," Santiago chuckled.

"Don't get too cocky," the President warned with the hint of a smile which turned grim when he asked, "What about this paramilitary group of his?"

"It's good news on this front also. We've uncovered this group and their leader and we are dealing with it," Santiago replied.

"And what, exactly, are we doing?"

"Mister President, it is probably best that you be kept out of the loop on this one. Please trust me when I tell you it is being taken care of," Santiago said.

"So be it, you've got my wink and a nod," it was one of the President's favorite phrases that Santiago had come to despise.

The President continued, "Paulo, I'd like to apologize for demanding your resignation the other day. I hope you understand it was something said in the heat of the moment. I trust you completely."

"Thank you, Mister President."

—

"That's him!" Corky cried, looking at a photo array placed before her on the desk in Sean Armstrong's house office. "I'm so sorry I forgot to record the video, but I swear that's him," she reiterated, placing her hands over her mouth.

"He's a thug and you did a good job just to get away from him, Corky," Ian said and continued, "and we believe he works for the President. You're safe now and that's what counts and you've been very helpful.

"I'm going to ask you to pack a bag and I'll ask my sister and her kids to do the same."

Corky tilted her head quizzically and then nodded and left the room.

Ian looked at Chalmers and then at his father and stated, "This house is no longer safe."

"How do you figure?" Chalmers asked.

"Because Long will put it together. He'll realize that night I made him in Lefty's was more than a coincidence. He knows about Mary's connection with Rusk and the GWI and he'll tie that together with the military style operation we conducted at their compound. It won't take him long to locate me."

"How do you know he'd tie that all together and come to that conclusion?" his father asked.

"Because I would have," Ian answered simply.

"Okay, so what should we do?" Chalmers asked.

"First we have to get our families and Corky out of harm's way and let Sol and George know of the new threat and that they need to increase their security. I think that you and your family should join my sister and her kids and go to Steve and Nancy's place. We'll send Grant and Jesse along for protection. Dad, I think you should join them too," Ian said.

"I'll stay here, thank you," Sean protested.

"Pop, I'm sorry, but you'll just get in the way. I mean no disrespect, but this isn't going to be like shooting skeet at the range," Ian explained.

"Son, this is my house and you're my son and I will stay and defend it and you," Sean said stubbornly.

"Ian, we'll send the families away, but I'm staying..." Chalmers started before Ian interrupted.

"Chuck, you have to think about your family..."

"Shut up, god dammit! Several years ago I accompanied you on a mission and saw it through. Since then we've been to hell and back and I've been there from start to finish and I know my wife and daughter would have had it no other way. If you think I'm not staying to see this through, you have another think coming!"

"God help me," Ian prayed and conceded, "I'm surrounded by a couple of stubborn old farts."

—

Chalmers' bravado began to diminish as he pulled into his driveway. He could stand up to Ian, but his wife was another matter. He was about to ask her and their daughter to disrupt their lives and go into hiding again. He thought sitting across the desk of a ruthless drug cartel king pin was easier than the task he now faced.

He opened the back kitchen door and was surprised to see Jennifer pulling a suitcase with a snow board tucked under her other arm approaching from the other side of the kitchen. She gave him a sly smile. She was followed into the room by her mother who was also pulling a piece of luggage.

"W-what...? Chalmers started.

"Save it, Chuck. I just got off the phone with Sheila," and turning to Jennifer she asked, "Did you pack your school books?"

"Yes, mother."

Colleen parked her suitcase, turned and briskly left the room.

"How much trouble am I in?" Chalmers asked his daughter.

"Big time trouble," Jennifer snickered and then concluded, "If I were you, I'd do some major ass kissing."

"Watch your mouth, young lady, and thanks," Chalmers moaned dutifully as he exited the room and walked down the hall.

He found Colleen in their bedroom with her back to him and packing a suitcase that was spread across the bed.

Chalmers stood in the doorway and meekly asked, "What about Jennifer's school?"

"Did you even think about that when you decided we needed to go into hiding, again?" Colleen demanded.

"Ahh…" Chalmers stammered.

"Never mind," Colleen said and continued, "Charles Raymond Chalmers," she started and Chalmers winced and thought, this is not a good sign, "the only other time I expected a promise from you is when you said, 'I do'. Now I want another promise from you.

"I want you to promise me that, after Jennifer graduates later this year, you will actually retire and we can spend our golden years doing things together and that you will let others save the world."

Chalmers walked over to Colleen and turned her around. He kissed her and hugged her and with his chin resting on her shoulder, whispered in her ear, "I do."

"Mary, some things have come up and you need to get to our place immediately," Ian said into the phone.

"Why Ian, since you put it so romantically, I'd love to visit you and your father, and thank you so much for asking, but oh my gosh, I just don't have anything to wear" Dinosa said bitter sweetly in a southern drawl.

"I apologize, but I'm serious. You're in danger again," Ian explained and as an afterthought, added, "If we're both going to die I'd like us to be together."

"Oh, Ian," she squealed, "You do have such a way with words and if you promise you'll make an honest woman of me, I'll be happy to accept your invitation."

"Fine," Ian replied.

"Oh Ian, I hope you don't feel coerced. You've made me the happiest maiden in the land with such a sweet proposal over," and her tone turned angry, "over the fucking phone!"

"Just get here…please?"

"Fine!"

Dinosa walked into Valerie Kane's office and plopped down on the couch.

"TGIFF," she groaned.

"I won't ask what the extra 'F' stands for," Kane replied.

"When did you know Nancy was the one for you?" Dinosa asked out of the blue.

Valerie looked curiously across her desk and said, "Ah, that dilemma, huh? Well, I can't really say. When we first met our relationship wasn't particularly politically correct. I suppose I realized she was the person I wanted to live with for the rest of my life and I didn't give a shit what others thought was the day I knew she was the one. I'm going to guess, you're referring to Ian O'Farrell. Did he propose?"

"Hell, I don't know. What scares me is, if he did, I think I'd accept," Dinosa mused.

"When you don't have to think about your answer, you'll know," Kane said.

"If you need me this weekend, I'll be spending it at Ian's place, and thanks Valerie."

As she exited the office, for some unknown reason, she recalled the pithy saying her Grandfather used to say, "When ifs and buts are candy and nuts, we'll all have a Merry Christmas."

Al Long and Peter McCoy sat inside a dark sedan parked on Market Street just a short distance from the parking garage adjacent to the Federal building and watched as Dinosa's Subaru pulled out of the garage and turn north. Long allowed a few cars to pass and then pulled out into traffic and followed her.

When she drove onto the northbound on the ramp to Route 101, he said, "Well, she ain't going home. I think she's going to see her boyfriend."

He maintained a few cars of separation as they crossed the Golden Gate Bridge and took the Sausalito exit. The sun had just set and brought with it a friendly darkness. They passed Dinosa as she turned off onto the lane that led to the O'Farrell estate.

Ian was at the bottom of the stairway to greet her as she pulled up and stopped. He extended his arms to greet her with a hug.

She brushed past him saying, "I was followed here. Ian, what the hell is going on?"

Not waiting for an answer she scurried up the stairs and Ian hurried after her.

Once inside, Ian started, "Everybody's in the…"

"The den, I know," Dinosa finished his sentence.

As they entered the den, Ian said, "Mary thinks she was followed here."

Dinosa glanced angrily at Ian and said, "I didn't say I thought I was followed here, I said I know I was followed. They never got close enough so I could identify them, but I think," and glancing at Ian she stressed the word 'think', "there were two men in a dark sedan."

Ian just shrugged and Chalmers said, "A little testy this evening, aren't we Dinosa?"

"Fuck you, Chuck! In the last week I've been mugged, drugged and knocked out. I've been kidnapped and dragged to bum fuck Iowa and locked in some god damned dungeon and then I had to baby sit some mind numbed women and children. And then, when I finally get home and all I want to do is crawl into a nice warm tub, you ass holes summon me here. You're fucking right I'm testy."

"Geez Dinosa, you're starting to sound a bit like an ankle," Chalmers remarked.

Dinosa remembered the day, back when she and Chalmers were partners working Homicide with the SFPD investigating the North Beach serial killer and when she had called a woman an 'ankle', she had to explain to Chalmers that she used that word in lieu of the 'C' word when referring to a woman that disgusted her. She explained it was more politically correct only, anatomically speaking, it was about two and a half feet lower.

Her nervous snicker turned to a hysterical guffaw and Chalmers joined her. Sean and his son looked at each other and just shrugged.

When the laughter subsided, Chalmers looked at Dinosa and chuckled, "And you were in bum fuck Idaho not Iowa."

"Okay, enough frivolity. What's the plan?" Sean asked.

"I don't believe he'll do anything tonight. He'll want to recon the grounds and the house first, but we still have to remain alert. He's probably out there now snooping around. I'm going to guess his partner is a fellow Green Beret, so they're both well trained and dangerous.

"He thinks he has the advantage of surprise and now we have that tactic on our side," Ian said.

He asked Mary, "Do you think you can identify the car?"

"I suppose if it was the only dark colored sedan among a bunch of pickups and SUVs, I could," Dinosa answered sarcastically.

"Ha, ha," Ian mumbled and turning toward his father asked, "The only overnight accommodations in town is the Casa Madrona Hotel, isn't it?"

"Other than a couple of Bed and Breakfasts, yes," Sean said.

"Okay, we'll take two hour shifts watching the security monitors and entry alerts. Like I said earlier, I don't think he'll strike tonight, but we still need to remain diligent," Ian said.

—

"As the debate grows over the President's use of armed drones in the recent attack on the Great White Nation in northern Idaho, so does the unrest on Capitol Hill. Joining us on 'D.C. Politics Tonight' is one of the men at the forefront of that debate, the junior Congressman from Oklahoma, Representative John Garcia. Welcome, Congressman."

"Good evening, Kathy, it's nice to be here," Garcia replied.

"What have you been able to uncover regarding the drone attack?"

"Well, the White House has been extremely tight lipped. We don't know a whole lot more than you do at this time," Garcia responded and continued, *"We do know that four drones were deployed by the Homeland Security Agency and were armed by that agency's authority. Many of us here on the Hill believe they have far exceeded their legal authority and the President has illegally abused his power by ordering a military attack on American citizens on American soil."*

"So where does your inquiry go from here?"

"A special session has been called for later tonight and the House Majority Leader, Congresswoman Sarah Peebles, will propose a bi-partisan committee be selected to investigate and

determine if any Homeland Security or Presidential illegal or inappropriate action was conducted in this matter," Garcia replied.

"Could that lead to Presidential impeachment?"

"Whoa, Kathy," Garcia laughed, *"Let's wait and see where that investigation takes us."*

President Benjamin clicked the off button on his television remote, looked across his desk in the 'Inner Chambers' at Paulo Santiago and asked calmly, "Okay, where do we stand?"

Santiago beamed and replied, "This will be the nail in their coffin. Our latest poll says the American people are squarely behind you. Sixty-eight percent approve your actions in destroying the GWN and your overall approval numbers have never been higher."

"God dammit Paulo, I hate it when you get so cocky," Benjamin said, raising his voice. "I mean, where will this House sub-committee lead?"

"That's what I'm trying to tell you, sir. Our speaking heads are already spinning this as just another feeble attempt on their part to discredit all the good you've accomplished. They turn it around and say, President Bush was prepared to use our Air Force to shoot down civilian commercial aircraft on nine eleven, for Christ's sake.

"Hell, you're a fucking American hero and they can't stand it!" Santiago exclaimed and added, "This anti-American campaign will lead to their party's ruin."

"What's the latest on Rusk and Corky?"

"Our best independent contractor is on it. He's traced the group to a house in Sausalito. California and he believes Corky Burmeister is there as well. It is best if you only know that the entire problem will be taken care of by tomorrow."

—

It was 4:00 am the next morning when Ian rolled his Vespa 150cc scooter out of the side door of the garage and wheeled it around to the front drive. Strapped over his back was a rectangular case about three feet in length. Dinosa peered from a second story window of the mansion and watched as he rounded a curve of the entrance lane and disappeared behind the tall oak trees. A feeling of dread fell over her and she whispered a little prayer.

Ian turned onto Rodeo Drive that would wind down the hill and take him to downtown Sausalito. He turned onto Bridge Way and drove the deserted street to the Casa Madrona Hotel and pulled down the alley next to the hotel entrance and the adjacent three story parking garage.

He parked his scooter in the alley and removed a thermos and a pair of night vision binoculars from a rear side compartment of the Vespa. He walked to the other side of the alley and boosted himself up a three foot retaining wall and sat down behind a row of oleander shrubs. From here he could see his scooter, but more importantly he had a clear view of the hotel's side exit that guests would take to the parking garage entrance and elevator.

He poured himself a cup of hot coffee from the thermos and leaned back against the trunk of a cypress tree. He glanced at his watch which read 4:20 am. A shuttle bus identified on the side as the 'Sausalito Chartered Fishing Parties' pulled into the alley and disappeared on its way to the hotel's main entrance. Five minutes later he saw two men emerge from the side exit of the hotel and stroll leisurely toward the parking garage, both carrying similar cases as the one draped over Ian's back.

He peered through the binoculars and whispered, "Bingo."

Ian jumped down from his perch and ran across the alley where he took up a position in the shadow of a building. A few minutes passed before a dark sedan emerged from the parking lot and turned into the alley. After it turned onto Bridge Way, Ian sprinted to his scooter and raced it down the alley.

He sped his way through back streets that would take him back to Rodeo Drive and he was sure he would beat the sedan back to the lane leading to his estate. When he arrived at the lane, he drove his scooter into the bushes and laid it down, hidden from passer byes.

He ran up the lane about fifty feet past the lighted entrance gate and hid among the oak and willow trees. He retrieved the two twenty-three sniper rifle from the case and decided he wouldn't need the attachable scope. He unfolded the stock and raised the weapon to his shoulder, chambering a round and clicking off the safety.

Movement from one of the monitors caught Dinosa's eye and attention. It came from the camera monitoring the gated entrance. She watched as a dark colored sedan with its lights off pull up to the gate and stop. Two men got out and walked to the rear of the car. One of the men produced two rifles from the trunk and handed one to his companion.

Without taking her eyes off of the monitor she hit a button on the console before her that would awaken and alert the sleeping Sean and Chalmers. She watched on the monitor as the two men walked toward the front of their car engaged is conversation.

Suddenly one of the men's head jerked back and he stumbled forward before falling to the ground. Before he hit the ground the other man fell to the ground. They both lay motionless. A minute later a man emerged on the screen walking cautiously toward the two downed men with his back toward the camera.

He bent down over the first body and felt for a pulse and then did the same to the other body. He stood up and fired another round into the second man, turned around and looking up at the camera, Ian gave the thumbs up sign.

"The son of a bitch will be hard to live with now," Dinosa sighed as a bleary eyed Chalmers entered the room.

The following morning Sean called his late wife's brother and Marin Country Chief medical examiner, Zacharias Peterson and said, "Zach, I have another favor to ask."

That evening's Marin County Herald newspaper contained the following story on page three ;

The Marin County Chief Medical Examiner, Doctor Zacharias Peterson has determined the blood discovered on a boat moored at Sausalito Marina was that of its missing owner, Ian Matthew O'Farrell and his friend Grant William Wilson.

According to police reports the two men were reported missing the previous night by O'Farrell's father, Sean O'Farrell of Sausalito, after they failed to return home following a planned fishing trip.

A police spokesman said the investigation surrounding the two missing men is still ongoing.

—

PART IV

Armageddon

The final battle of God versus the Devil

CHAPTER SEVENTEEN

The four men trudged in line up the bank of the west fork of the Priest River through the tall grass and leafing huckleberry bushes. Each carried a fly fishing rod and the trailing two shared toting each end of an ice chest. They followed a rough path back to a roadside turnout where their Humvee waited.

The sky was clear and a slight breeze chilled the early Spring day. They stowed their fishing gear and ice chest in the back and then loaded themselves into the vehicle.

As Joshua started the engine he boasted, "God has been kind to us today rewarding us with a good catch. Tonight we will feast on a mighty fine supper."

They made the short trip back to 'Heaven's Gate' and their river bank cabin. That evening they did indeed feast on rainbow trout with a side of pork and beans and corn bread. When they had cleaned up the dinner dishes they retired to the comfortable confines of the small living room.

Joshua produced four binders and handed each of the others one and settling into an easy chair, said, "Okay boys, we've gone over this repeatedly, but we're getting' close to 'D-Day' and we'll be reviewing this daily until we depart next week. Boys, Armageddon is nigh!"

The front page headline in the Washington Tribune read;

RENEGADE MEMBERS OF THE 'GWN' THREATENS ARMAGEDDON
Homeland Security Questions Validity of Threat

"God damn it! What the hell is going on?!" President Benjamin demanded, slamming the newspaper down on his desk.

Gathered with him in the Oval Office was his Chief of Staff, Paulo Santiago, the director of the FBI and the Secretary of Homeland Security and the U.S. Attorney General.

"Is there any truth to this?" Santiago asked, shifting the blame to the Director of the FBI.

"We're looking into it. There is the chance several of their members may have left the compound prior to the attack, although we haven't uncovered any facts to back up that claim.

"Had we been included early on and involved with the planning, I can confidently say we wouldn't be having this conversation," Henry said, looking dubiously at the Homeland Security Secretary.

"Don't look at me. My orders came directly from this office," the Secretary replied defensively, pointing the proverbial finger back at Santiago.

The President buried his face in his hands and mumbled, "Why do I feel like I'm trying to have an intelligent conversation with the three stooges?"

"Henry, bring this reporter in and get every bit of information possible from him. We know who his 'reliable, inside Washington source' is, but we need to know everything he knows," Santiago said.

"There's a little thing protected by the U.S. Constitution called the freedom of the press," Henry replied.

"I don't give a shit if you have to pull all of his finger nails out! This is a matter of national security!" Santiago exploded.

—

The Justice Foundation members and Bernard Rusk were gathered in the theater room at the Armstrong home.

"We all agree that whatever this Armageddon might mean, it will happen soon. Yesterday was the first day of Spring and we know from the intelligence we recovered, it could happen anytime now.

"This Joshua Johnson refers to it as an event that will make nine eleven seem like a mosquito bite. He makes reference to the heathens that make a mockery of God's law and that they shall writher in a slow painful death of their own making.

"We have found nothing to indicate an actual venue or planning for this attack. The best analysts we have, including our own Doctor Tanaka, have reviewed the material we have and the only thing they have agreed on is that it will occur in the San Francisco Bay Area and they have a local benefactor supplying them with a safe house. We're assuming they have additional outside help and support."

"Well, if they plan on making nine eleven look like a mosquito bite, we should be looking at a large scheduled event. The Giants open the season on April second at AT&T Park. There would be over fifty thousand people there," Chalmers contributed.

"Yes, we've considered that and so has everybody else. Local law enforcement, the FBI and Homeland Security have been briefed. My sources say the White House is still denying the threat, but you can bet the farm, no pun intended, they'll be covering their asses. Homeland Security has been put on high alert and we've provided every law enforcement agency in the country the name of Frank 'Joshua' Johnson along with Doctor Tanaka's aged enhanced pictures and that he may be accompanied by three or four younger companions.

"Unfortunately, across the nation everybody is concerned that Armageddon will happen in their back yard and all of the police authorities are spread thin," Rusk replied and continued, "Our best efforts should be directed on determining where, how and when it will take place."

Ian stood up and said, "What could they have in their arsenal that could cause a disaster on such a large scale as they're describing? Could they have acquired a dirty nuclear device?"

The room went eerily silent as everyone contemplated the question posed and its' horrifying implications.

—

Snoopy entered the loft bedroom of the cabin she shared with her husband in the Santa Cruz Mountains and sat a cup of hot tea on the desk where Grub was studying information displayed on his computer monitor.

"Honey," she said wrapping her arms around his shoulders and standing behind him, "Take a break. You've been pouring over this stuff for days now."

Grub took his eyes off the monitor and looked up at his wife and smiling replied, "Snoops, if Ian is right and they have a dirty bomb, it could be devastating."

"How devastating?" Snoopy asked.

"Well, that depends on the size of the bomb and when and where it's detonated. Let's say it's a suitcase bomb and is full of cobalt uranium pellets or other radioactive dirty materiel and thirty or forty pounds of C-4 explosives and it goes off in AT&T Park on opening day. Depending on where it's located inside the park, the explosion itself could kill and maim thousands and the radiation would certainly contaminate those people in the park.

"If the prevailing westerly wind is normal for this time of the year, the radiation cloud would reach Oakland and the San Jose basin with an hour. The immediate and long term effects could eventually cost the lives and health of millions."

Snoopy rested her chin on her husband's head and sighed, "My God, could anyone do such a thing? Honey, you're exhausted to the point of diminishing returns. For everybody's sake, you need to get some rest."

Grub moaned, "You're right," closed his eyes and began to relax when suddenly he jolted up to Snoopy's surprise and cried out, "Holy crap! I've got to call Ian."

—

The Humvee pulled up to the gate at the end of the paved lane in Clayton, California and Joshua rolled the window down and showed his face to the camera mounted atop a post. The gate swung open and he drove through and to a circular driveway and parked in front of a magnificent two story sprawling home.

Standing at the bottom of the home's entrance was man a slightly younger than Joshua and who bore a remarkably resemblance to him. He approached Joshua with open arms and hugging him said, "Oh brother Frank, it's so good to see ya. I never believed this day would ever come."

Joshua returned the hug and then stepped back and said, "It's good to see you, too brother Robert, and its Joshua now."

"Oh yeah, I forgot and you can call me Bob."

Introductions were made and the group followed Bob into his residence where his wife met them.

"Joshua," Bob said, "This is my wife, Gretchen."

"Nice to meet you ma'am," Joshua said. "Sure is a nice big spread ya'll got here."

"Does seem a bit large since the kids grew up and all moved away," Gretchen replied.

"Well, come on in and sit a spell. We've got the guest house all set up for your boys and Gretchen's prepared the guest bedroom here in the house for you," Bob said.

"That's real cordial of you Bob, but I'd prefer staying with my men, if you don't mind."

"Suit yourself," Bob said escorting the group into a large living room.

After they had all settled into easy chairs, Bob asked, "How long you figure you'll be stayin'?"

"Oh, not more than a week or so," Joshua replied.

"You know Frank, I would've given my left gonad if I could have joined you and the others when you left Hayfork years ago," Bob said.

"I know, but you were a bit young it those days," Joshua said.

"Well, I know you can't tell me what you guys are up to, but I've done my best to support the movement our Daddy set up. The other boys you sent here left a powerful message for the heathens that live in these parts," Bob exclaimed.

"Yes, brother Bob, you've been a blessing sent from God and you will be rewarded," Joshua said standing up and added, "We've had a tiring trip and we'd be mighty thankful if you could show us the way to the guest house. We can catch up later."

—

CHAPTER EIGHTEEN

"Ian, its Grub," he said excitedly, "We've got to get back to the house at the compound!"

"Whoa, slow down. First tell me what you found," Ian replied, sharing Grub's enthusiasm with anticipation.

"Joshua's plan is buried under the basement," Grub blurted out.

"How do you…" Ian started.

"I downloaded every word of Joshua's writings and processed them through an analysis program I wrote. The word 'plan' appeared in some form forty-two times. The words 'House of Asher' appeared eighteen times and the word 'underground' appeared thirty-three times.

"We know the farm house was referred to as the 'House of Asher' and I presumed 'underground' meant the team had to go underground to covertly accomplish the plan. But, the frequency of these words appearing in his writing couldn't be a coincident.

"I couldn't get these words out of my head and then it hit me. I went back in my mind and remembered one passage that, at the time I first read it, didn't make a lot of sense. It said, 'should our mission fail, survivors should return to the 'House of Asher', pray to the Lord and the underground plan shall be revealed.'

"Ian, the plan has to be buried underground at the 'House of Asher'."

"Wow," Ian said, his mind running in overdrive. He turned toward Mary, lying next to him and asked, "Do you remember what the floor in the basement at the home you were being held captive was made of?"

"What are you talking about?" Dinosa replied dumbfounded.

"Was it concrete, wood or dirt?"

"Geez, let me think," she paused and then said, "I think it was wood. No, wait a minute, that was the fire wood shack floor. The basement floor was dirt. I remember because I had to brush off my feet before I put my shoes on."

"Well, when are we leaving?" Grub asked from the other end of the line.

Ian replied, "How sure are you, Grub?"

"Oh for crying out loud, Ian, I could run it through a probability program, but trust me on this. The Lord of cyberspace does not lie."

"Okay, but I'm afraid you can't go. We need you here doing your thing. This is our arena and we'll take it from here, but Grub, you may have just saved thousands of lives," Ian said.

Ian hung of the phone and immediately dialed Solomon Goldsmith.

"Hey Sol, its Ian," he said into the phone, "Can you get away for a day or two? We need you and your plane."

"Yeah sure, where we going?"

"Back to Bonners Ferry."

"When?"

"Now."

"See ya at the field in an hour."

Ian's next call was to Chuck Chalmers.

—

"That yellow bellied, cock sucking traitor!" Santiago bellowed, "We got the son of a bitch elected!"

Paulo Santiago was sitting across the desk from President Barrymore Benjamin in the 'Inner Sanctum' of the White House. They were watching the television and the House of Representative's vote to impeach the President of the United

States was broadcasting live. Santiago's outburst was in response to Congressman Wilbur Madison's 'aye' vote.

"Well, that settles it," Benjamin chuckled, "I've just become the third President in the country's history to be impeached. See to it a personal thank you note is sent to all the 'nay' voters and make sure party funds to Wilbur are cut off."

Santiago peered quizzically at his boss and asked, "Doesn't this concern you?"

"Hell no, I'm honored. Old Bill Clinton was impeached and he's now hailed as one of our nation's most beloved presidents. Richard Nixon was a coward and resigned before congress could impeach him and look how history has treated him. Paulo, I am no coward. This represents a challenge that will only bolster my legacy."

Santiago returned his bosses smile, but deep down he was crushed to think he had faithfully followed this man only to discover now that he's a self-absorbed, narcissistic maniac.

"Paulo, I want you to schedule with the news media and television networks a Presidential address to the nation for prime time tonight and have the FBI arrest Bernard Rusk."

—

Bonners Ferry Chief of Police, Dwight MacArthur greeted Chalmers, Ian and Sol as they deplaned at the county air field.

"Good to see you, Chuck. How's our little Dinosa doing?" Mack said.

"She's healed quite well, but if she heard you say 'our little Dinosa', I'm sure you wouldn't be fairing as well. I've been told it's hard to remove your nuts from your throat," Chalmers chuckled.

After sharing a laugh, Mack said, "Well, I stopped at the compound a little while ago and the only security I could detect was two FBI agents at the gate. I chatted with them and they were pretty tight lipped. One of them mentioned the cleanup had begun and what was left of the house had been bull dozed up into a pile and the county fire department was scheduled to burn it tomorrow and the basement hole would be filled with dirt sometime next week."

"Thank you Mack, I guess we better get moving," Chuck said, turning to the others who were already unloading gear from the plane's cargo hold and loading it into a rental van. Among several crates was one labeled 'MULD (Mobile Ultrasonic Locating Device)'.

When they finished loading the van, Chalmers walked up to Mack and again shaking his hand said, "Mack I want you to know how much we appreciate your help. When this is all done I'd like to sit down and have a long conversation with you so I can explain everything."

Mack smiled, cocked his head and said, "Hey, trout season opens on Memorial Day. Why don't you and Colleen come up and visit. I know some great fly fishing streams."

"We just might take you up on that," Chalmers replied.

The team loaded into the van and drove off the air strip and through town and directly to the compound. Chalmers thought they had about three hours of good sun light left. They pulled up to the gate and stopped. Sol jumped out of the passenger seat and pulled out a shoulder mounted camcorder and a tote bag from behind the seat and Chalmers emerged from the driver's side holding a clip board.

The two FBI agents approached with their hands on their holsters and their badges visible. The shorter of the two demanded, "Hold it right there, partner. FBI, may I ask your business here?"

"Yes of course, agents," Chalmers started and continued, "My name is Dave Kaufman and this is my producer Michael O'Brien. We're an independent news team doing a piece on the aftermath of the Great White Nation and wanted to get some shots of the compound and maybe interview you two."

The two agents relaxed some and the taller one said, "I'm afraid that won't be possible, sir. No unauthorized personnel are allowed beyond this point."

Ian stepped out from behind the van with an AR16 assault rifle leveled on the two agents and as they both gestured toward their side arms, he hollered, "Don't even think about it or your names will be on a wall in the Hoover Building."

Chalmers stepped forward and removed the agents side arms and ankle backups. Sol stepped up and opened his tote bag and Chalmers removed a syringe from it. He turned and jabbed the needle in the tall agent's neck, holding him up with his other arm. The agents stumbled and his body went slack.

The other agent turned and ran. Ian fired a short burst and the dust flew around the fleeing man's feet. He stopped abruptly and froze.

"Hey, pal," Chalmers said, "This isn't lethal. It'll just knock you out for a while and you'll wake up with a hell of a hangover, but you'll still be alive."

After injecting the second agent they loaded the two men into the rear of the van and proceeded up the road to what was left of the compound. A large pile of gravel and a large pile of dirt sat next to a hole in the ground where the farm house had once been.

A bull dozer was located a short distance away.

"Looks like we were none too soon," Sol said as they exited the van.

The floor of the basement was left pretty much in tact except the floor was littered with clothing shreds, splintered wood, dirt and rock. A partially demolished stairway led to a one time landing of the first floor Work benches lined one of the footing walls and the cot Dinosa described as her bed sat in one corner. The wood stove was in the opposite corner with crushed flues partially covering it. Beside it and extending at a diagonal was the crumpled metal wood shaft that had once provided Dinosa an escape route.

The three men unloaded the van and descended into the hole with the MULD, several shovels and a pry bar. Chalmers walked immediately to the area under the stairway and started clearing an access to the area. Sol and Ian were busy uncrating the MULD when Chalmers cried, "Bingo, you guys can forget the MULD."

The two hustled over to where Chalmers was lifting a metal cover from the floor beneath the stairwell revealing a cubby hole buried in the dirt containing a small metal box which he withdrew. Excitingly he backed out and tripped over a piece of fallen timber and landed ungracefully on his ass with the metal box in his lap. "Son of a bitch," he complained.

Sol and Ian crowded around him as he opened the container. Underneath twenty one hundred dollar bills, Chalmers removed a note book. As he leafed through it, Ian took pictures of each page with his I-phone.

"Let me get these off to Grub and the rest of the team and let's get the hell out of here," Ian exclaimed.

—

"Dammit Paulo, where are the Senator and Congressman?" the President demanded as they walked through the back stage door to the West Wing Assembly Hall of the White House.

"Well," Santiago stammered, "The Senator took suddenly ill and I'm told the Congressman is stuck in traffic."

Santiago was instructed to have the Senate Majority Leader and the House Minority Leader present to stand behind the President during the press conference.

"Those chicken shit bastards, how's it going to look if the leaders of my own party aren't here to support me? Believe me, they will be sorry," Benjamin stated under his breath.

President Benjamin strode confidently with his chin held high and jutting and stood behind the dais and in front of the Attorney General, the Director of the FBI and his Chief of Staff on the stage facing the camera and audience.

"Ladies and Gentlemen, my fellow citizens, as your elected President and Commander In Chief, I am announcing tonight that my Attorney General, Agambi Pequod, has requested and been granted from a Washington, D.C. federal judge, a warrant for the arrest of Deputy Director of the CIA, Bernard Rusk, charging him with high treason against the United States of America, conspiracy to overthrow our government, conspiracy to murder and sixteen other related charges," the President began.

"I've further ordered he be placed under arrest by agents of the FBI. I've been informed by the FBI that Mr. Rusk has not been located and is presumed to be on the run or in hiding. Agents of the FBI and U.S. Marshall Service are currently chasing down leads as to his location and I've been informed his arrest is imminent.

"I'm asking Mr. Rusk, if he is watching, he can end this man hunt by simply turning himself in and facing these accusations before a court of law."

The President paused and raised his head and scanned the silent audience. He squinted slightly and looked intently into the single television camera shared by the media and continued, "My fellow Americans, I can say I make this announcement with a heavy heart, but I ask you, once again, to put your trust in me. Grave injustices have been perpetrated against our Nation and this White House with the intent to disunite us as a country and a people. I give you my word I will not allow this to happen. Arrest warrants for other people involved with Mr. Rusk's conspiracy have been issued and more are presently being prepared.

"This period of time of our Nation's history will be recorded as a low point, but I promise you, it will not destroy the greatest nation that has ever been," his voice began to rise in volume as he continued, "We will stand up and crush this tyranny and this nation, born in a revolution against a tyrannical ruler and survivor of a civil war and two world wars, shall prevail against this futile attempt to usurp and disrupt the greatest democratic free nation the world has ever seen! Thank you for your support, and may God bless America!"

To the rousing applause of the hastily gathered audience, the President turned and marched off of the stage.

—

"We don't have much time," Bernard Rusk addressed the team gathered in the O'Farrell manor theater room.

He continued, "After analyzing the documents we retrieved from the basement at the compound, Grub has calculated a ninety percent probability that the GWN's target is the 'Gay and Lesbian Freedom Front International' annual convention to be held at Candlestick Park in Hunters Point this weekend. It will be attended by over one hundred thousand gays and lesbians and their supporters and the opening ceremony is tomorrow starting at noon.

"If Grub puts a ninety percent probability factor on this, I put it at one hundred percent. I believe we have to concentrate our interdiction efforts on this target. That gives us a little over twenty-four hours until zero hour can occur and we only know it will occur sometime this weekend.

"Now some good news; you've all been given a packet with a series of computer age enhanced photographs of a photo taken of Frank Johnson when he was in his early twenties. They show what Frank or Joshua would look like today in various stages of beard growth. We know he is accompanied by three or four others we presume are younger men, but we have no idea of who they are and what they look like.

"We are in the process of installing cameras at each turnstile and service entrance to the park which will take a snapshot of each individual that enters. Those pictures will be processed through a facial recognition program and if he enters the park we should be alerted.

"Since we've identified Mr. Johnson's family, I've had my people doing a trace of other family members. All have been accounted for and their whereabouts are known except for one of his brothers, Robert Johnson. It seems this guy moved west from Alabama about twenty years ago and relocated in the Bay Area. We're following leads and should have his address any time now. We have to assume he is an accomplice.

"Now, more bad news; we presumed any dirty nuclear waste would have been procured through the international black market and smuggled in from a foreign country where nuclear waste is not meticulously monitored. However, the astute Mr. Tanaka asked just how fail safe our country's monitoring and accountability of nuclear waste is.

"So, we conducted an independent audit on this country's four nuclear waste facilities and discovered one, a plant outside of Elko, Nevada, could not account for a little over one hundred pounds of nuclear reactor pellets that have a half-life of eighty years. They were reported missing about three months ago and, believe it or not, the report somehow got lost at the NEC and no action has been taken.

"I'm told, this is enough nuclear waste that if released with enough force from Hunters Point, would contaminate the East and South Bay Area with secondary exposure to the San Joaquin and Sacramento Valleys. It would result in literally millions of casualties."

Everyone's attention was diverted to Chad Carbahol as he entered the theater.

"Hope I'm not here too late. I came as soon as I got your word, Bernie," he said taking a seat next to Ian.

"Not at all, Chad, you made pretty good time, I'd say," Rusk replied.

"I've asked Chad to be here," Rusk continued, "because he's the Director of Security for the GALFFI and is heading up internal security for the group at Candlestick Park."

The group all looked at Chad with surprise and Mary Dinosa remarked, "Unbelievable."

"Don't look so surprised," Chad chuckled. "I got tired of the military's 'don't ask, don't tell' policy and resigned from the Army. Mr. Rusk offered me a position as a private contractor for his agency and I accepted. And yes, I'm a card carrying member of the GALFFI."

"No offense, Chad, I'm just thinking of all the broken hearted young ladies," Dinosa said with a rare blush.

"So, what have we learned?" Chad asked, ignoring Dinosa's remark.

Rusk filled him in and brought him up to date and Carbahol looked confused and asked, "Have you alerted all the proper authorities of this?"

"If by proper authorities you mean the FBI, DHLS or local law officials, no we haven't," Rusk said and continued, "We haven't yet located these assholes and have no idea where the dirty bomb is. If we involve the feds, it would be a cluster fuck. If the GWN believe we're close they could detonate the bomb anywhere. At least we know their intended target and we're working on finding their location.

"Chad, I would strongly urge you to speak with your conventions planers and leadership and recommend they cancel this weekend's activities."

Rusk was interrupted by his text alert and holding up a finger he peered at his telephone.

"Great," he addressed the group, "We've got an address for Johnson's brother. He lives in Clayton, California. Ian, a chopper is standing by and you and your team can be on site in forty-five minutes. We'll give you more information when you're in the air."

Ian turned toward Jesse and Grant and said, "Let's saddle up."

—

Robert stood on his porch with his arm around his wife Gretchen and as they both waved at the rear of the Humvee as it disappeared around the corner at the end of their drive he said, "God speed, Joshua."

Less than an hour later the Humvee pulled into the driveway and the garage of a hillside home in South San Francisco. The four men exited the vehicle and entered the house through a garage access door.

At the same time the helicopter carrying Ian, Jesse and Grant sat down on the football field at Clayton Valley High School. A black SUV with its driver was waiting for them as they unloaded their gear.

The young man approached the three men and said, "My name is Daniel Galloway and I've been ordered by Mr. Rusk to meet you. I've located the Johnson home and have satellite images of the area. What are your orders?"

"Well, first let's get out of here. Is there a more private area nearby?"

"Yes sir," Galloway replied.

They loaded their gear in the back of the SUV and drove off the campus and to an abandoned rock quarry not far away. Galloway got out, grabbing a key ring and walked to the gate. Trying several keys he found the right one and unlocked and swung open the gate. They drove onto the grounds and pulled up next to a run-down shack and the four men exited the vehicle. Carrying their gear and maps they entered the shack and Galloway spread the satellite map of the area on a table.

Pointing to a location on the map, Galloway said, "This is the Johnson home and this is where we are."

Moving his finger he added, "This is a State Park's road that accesses the north side of Mount Diablo State Park."

The road he was pointing at was accessible from the south side of the quarry and circled around to the top of a hill with a clear elevated view less than two hundred yards from the Johnson residence. They exited the shack and piled back into the SUV and drove the park road to the top of the hill.

They crouched down and peered down on the Johnson home through binoculars. The home sat on an isolated half acre lot at the end of a private lane. It was a ranch style, two story home with an attached garage and a guest house at the back of the property. The rear of the home faced a kidney shaped swimming pool. The property was surrounded by a rail fence.

"I don't see any perimeter security," Grant said.

"All right, everybody button up and let's make sure our communications are working," Ian said.

Everyone retrieved a transceiver button and inserted it in their ear. After checking to make sure they could hear each other, Ian calmly said, "Grant, you stay here and set up the AR72 and watch our back. Jesse, you and I will circle down and approach the house from that grove of walnut trees to the south."

"What do you want me to do?" Galloway asked anxiously.

"You wait here and stay low. When it's over, drive Grant and meet us at the house," Ian replied.

"Hey, I'm a field agent you know," Galloway whined.

"Then follow orders," Ian growled, thinking the kid still had peach fuzz on his chin.

Ian and Grant crouched down in the tall grass and made their way down the hill side. When they emerged from the orchard they found themselves at the rail fence about ten yards from the side of the garage.

"Jesse, are you set?" Ian spoke softly.

"Ten-four," came the response.

"Grant, you take the back door and I'll take the front. Jesse, keep an eye on the guest house," Ian said.

Grant jumped the fence and ran to the back door and took a position next to the double glass door with his pistol raised to his chest. Ian followed him over the fence and ran first to the garage window and peeked in. He saw two late model BMWs parked side by side.

"His and her beamers in the garage, let's hope they're the only ones here," Ian said.

He made his way slowly around the front of the garage and to the front door. Stuffing his hand gun between his trousers in the small of his back, he said, "Everybody, stand-by."

He rang the front door bell and listened to a series of chimes. A minute later an elderly woman resembling Aunt

Bea from the Andy Griffin show answered and said sweetly, "May I help you?"

"Yes Ma'am, is Mister Johnson home?" Ian asked.

"I'm right here," Johnson said gruffly walking up behind his wife. He continued, "What do you want?"

Ian produced the gun from behind his back and stepping into the room said calmly, "Just a word with you."

"What the hell do you think you're doing, young man?" Johnson protested.

"Just sit down, shut up and listen and you might live through this," Ian responded, motioning the couple back into their living room, "Take a seat," he ordered.

"Who else is here?" Ian demanded.

"Nobody...I, I swear there's nobody else hear," Gretchen moaned.

"'Grant, come in and clear the house. Jesse, stay put," Ian said.

"What the hell do you want!" Robert said with false bravado.

"Where is your brother, Frank or Joshua or whatever you call him?" Ian asked calmly.

"I don't have a brother," Robert retorted.

"Do you have any idea what he's up to? Do you realize he's about to release a dirty bomb that will spread deadly radiation that will kill and maim millions for the next forty years or more?" He looked at Gretchen and pleaded, "Do you have children and grandchildren that live in the Bay Area? This man is willing to sacrifice the ones you love for some sick mission. Are you willing to protect this maniac?"

Gretchen looked at Robert and said, "What's he talking about?"

"Misses Johnson, you're old enough to remember the fall out effect on the Japanese people after we bombed Hiroshima and Nagasaki and the affect the nuclear plant disaster in the Ukraine has had on their people now for generations. That's what your brother-in-law has planned for the Bay Area," Ian spat out.

Gretchen looked incredulously at her husband and moaned, "Bob, is this true?"

"He's bluffing," Johnson sneered. "He couldn't possibly know Frank's plan. Hell, we don't even know his plan."

"You're wrong!" Ian yelled and slapped Johnson across his face.

"How do you think we traced him here? How did we find and destroy the compound in Idaho? We know his target, we know his plan and we know he's intent on carrying it out. You are already guilty of aiding and abetting criminal and terrorist acts for the Synagogue bombing in San Francisco and the Church gassing in Oakland.

"Are you willing to be guilty of assisting in the worst slaughter of innocent people in our Nation's history. I'm going to ask you one last time, where is your brother?"

Johnson wiped his face and looked down dejectedly.

"For heaven's sake, Robert, tell him," his wife pleaded.

"I know they have a safe house in South San Francisco. I don't know the address, but I do know he goes under the alias of Joshua Mathew and they're driving a black Humvee," Johnson groaned.

Grant entered the room and said, "The house is clear."

"Jesse, get down here ASAP," Ian said.

Ian next called Rusk and passed along the information he had just learned and after a brief conversation he escorted the Johnsons into the dining room and handcuffed them together around either side of a corner post at a counter that separated the room from the kitchen.

He and Grant then proceeded to the front porch where Jesse and Galloway pulled up in front of them. Ian walked to the driver's side and opened the door.

"Out," he simply said and handed Galloway a key.

Begrudgingly Galloway exited the vehicle and asked, "What's this?"

"The key to the handcuffs attached to the elderly couple inside. I need you to keep an eye on them," Ian replied.

"For how long?" Galloway questioned.

"Until you're relieved or you get further orders," and as he put the car in drive to pull away Ian added, "You did a good job today, Calloway."

"That's Galloway, sir!" the young man yelled over the squeal of the tires as the SUV sped off down the lane.

—

FBI Senior Field Agent Jack Jackson sat in the passenger seat of a dark sedan peering through binoculars at the home on the end of Ashley Court on a hillside overlooking the industrial district of South San Francisco and the bay. Beside him and behind the wheel sat Mary Dinosa and in the back seat was Valerie Kane.

"I hope your credible, anonymous source is right. If this operation goes south, we're going to look like fools," Jackson remarked.

Dinosa thought that wouldn't be unusual for old 'Acton Jackson', but kept her mouth shut.

The three were monitoring the SWAT team communications as two armored personnel carriers pulled up in front of the home and their rear doors swung open. A dozen team members dressed in full body armor and armed with fully automatic rifles filed out of both vehicles. The six man entry team approached the front door while the remaining members surrounded the house.

"On my three count, two, one, go!" cackled over the radio as four flash bomb grenades were tossed and crashed through various windows of the house.

A moment later the ram hit the front door and the six man entry team disappeared into the house.

"FBI, FBI, everybody on their stomachs with your hands in the air!" was heard over the radio followed by a series of, "Clear…clear…clear."

A few agonizing minutes later the radio cackled again, "The residence is clear and apparently vacated. Mobile command, no subjects found."

Jackson's head sagged and he groaned, "Shit, shit…"

He exited the car and walked briskly toward the house. Dinosa started the car and spun a U-turn and sped off.

From the back seat Kane chuckled, "Are you just going to leave him there?"

"Call it pay back," Dinosa smiled and added, "Besides I didn't think you'd want to be here when the press arrives."

—

In the basin industrial area below the SWAT raid a Budweiser tractor trailer rig pulled out of the beer distributer's parking lot and made a left turn onto Industrial Boulevard and two blocks later pulled up behind a black Humvee stopped at an intersection.

When the Humvee didn't pull forward after the cross traffic cleared, the driver of the beer truck turned toward his partner and barked, "What the fuck is this asshole waiting for!?"

Suddenly two casually dressed men got out of the Humvee and strolled back to the truck's cab. One walked to the passenger side and the other approached the driver.

"Sorry, but we seemed to be stalled," he said as the driver rolled down his window.

"Shit," the driver said, starting to shift into reverse.

When he turned his head to look in the rear view mirror he found himself staring down the barrel of a pistol. Simultaneously the passenger door swung open and the other man said calmly while pressing a hand gun against the passenger's temple, "Get on the floor."

Opening the driver's door, the other intruder said, "Scoot over."

"Hey man, we don't carry any cash," the driver protested.

"Just shut up and move!" the man growled as he jumped into the cab behind the steering wheel.

They followed the Humvee across the intersection and turned down an alley between two deserted warehouses and parked in the lot behind. The two Budweiser employees were ordered out of the truck and escorted through a door into the bay of the warehouse.

The two terrified men stood shivering in the middle of the room with pistols pointed at each of their heads when an elderly man sporting a long and wild white beard addressed them, "Please, disrobe."

"No way, man," the driver said, his quivering voice betraying his bravado.

The bearded man nodded at one of the men holding a hand gun and the man slammed the barrel of his pistol across the driver's forehead. He yelped and dropped to one knee.

"I said, disrobe, please," the bearded man repeated.

When the two men were stripped to their underwear the bearded man nodded again and two shots later their dead bodies lay on the cold warehouse floor.

One of the younger men gathered the two dead men's company ID tags and walked to a desk where he sat down and turned on a lamp. With razor knife he expertly removed the photos from the cards and replaced them with photos of his two young friends. He walked back to the group and handed each of the two men who had changed into the dead men's clothing an ID tag.

The large slide up door at the rear of the building was hoisted up and the Budweiser truck backed into the opened bay. The hydraulic lift gate on the rear of the truck was lowered and three Budweiser beer kegs were loaded into the van of the truck.

Joshua looked solemnly at his three young followers and said, "Take a knee and lets us pray...Oh Lord in Heaven deliver us from this task, in your name, we are now ready to embark on. Give us the courage and the strength to rid our world of those most guilty of defiling your will. Men who lay down with other men shall be put to death and so the same fate shall befall those who condone it."

—

CHAPTER NINETEEN

"Well, Bernie, how does it feel to be the most wanted person in the United States?" George Armstrong asked with a hint of sarcasm.

The two were lounging on the back deck with the home's owner, Sean O'Farrell.

"I don't believe my father would be proud, but seriously, I'll turn myself in as soon as we deal with this Great White Nation, or what's left of it," Rusk replied.

"Out of curiosity, how and what motivated you to get involved in all of this?" Sean asked.

"Well, it certainly wasn't because I thought I was the chosen one that's for sure. I guess it goes back to my younger years during the Viet Nam conflict when I first joined the CIA as a dumb and naïve rookie agent. I obeyed orders and carried out some questionable black ops out of a sense of duty in those days.

"After the war, I was relocated back to D.C. and lived through and witnessed politics at its worst. The Nixon Administration was corrupt and Watergate was just the surface of the iceberg. I also witnessed some very courageous men step forward and put an end to it. They were my inspiration. One particular man, one not too different from you two gentlemen, took me under his wing and introduced me to other like patriots. They shall all remain nameless, but they put me in a position to gather information on evil or potentially evil men and women that presented a threat to our form of government.

"Since then, I've lived and worked under seven Administrations and along with a few others, who will also go unnamed, we have compiled many dossiers filed under this category. Over the years we have discovered many abuses, but so far, we have used this information only when we found it necessary to protect the interests and security of our country and we have managed to maintain our anonymity. You may recall the resignation of the Senate Oversight Chairman and the Director of the FBI stepping down.

"The efforts of your 'Justice Foundation' have been pivotal in bringing down many of the outrageously abusive politicians and government officials.

"Like my mentor and his friends we have recently decided we must come out of the closet. This current Administration is the largest and most widespread criminal activity and abuse of power we've ever seen and we plan on exposing it. It'll get real ugly because at the top is President Benjamin, although we've discovered some time ago that he is but a mere puppet.

"He was handpicked years ago and his fate was predetermined by some people intent on over throwing our form of government. They were and are a group of radical black, mostly Muslim men and women, highly intelligent individuals, who realized it would take generations to become the majority in this country. They have used any, and I mean any tactic to achieve their goals that include assassination and subversion. The guilt and sense of fair play of the American electorate have allowed them to get away with it. They must be stopped and to accomplish that we have to expose ourselves," he concluded.

"How do you propose to do this," Sean asked.

"I can only tell you our plan calls for limited innocent casualties and your group will be protected from any legal prosecutions. In essence, your people will be given immunity for the information you can provide," Rusk replied.

—

President Benjamin slid a manila envelope across his desk in the 'Sanctuary' to his Chief of Staff, Paulo Santiago and said, "This is a list of men and women that must be silenced and I mean permanently. I don't care how it's done, I just want it done. Feel free to add any names to the list you feel appropriate."

Santiago looked haggard and disheveled with a day's growth of beard and dark circles under his blood shot eyes. A tear trickled down his cheek as he slouched in his chair facing his Commander in Chief.

"Paulo, you look terrible. You really should get more sleep. When this is over, I'm going to insist you take a long relaxing vacation."

Santiago didn't pick up the envelope. He struggled to his feet and through tearing eyes he cried, "Mister President, I'm afraid it is over. The 'Brotherhood' has informed me you no longer have their support. They suggest you start working on your letter of resignation. You'll have mine on your desk before the end of the day."

He turned around and with his head down, walked out of the room.

—

The Budweiser truck pulled up to the service entrance security check point at Candlestick Park. The driver and his partner were ordered by one of the security guards to get out of the cab. The security guard was accompanied by his partner, a uniformed SFPD Officer with his bomb sniffing German Shepard and two other men wearing windbreakers identifying themselves as FBI Agents.

The two Budweiser employees were asked to hand over their employee IDs and one of the FBI Agents ran them through a hand-held scanning device. After a green light appeared on the device he asked the men to open the rear of their van.

The dog was given the command by his handler and he jumped into the van and circled the cargo of fifty beer kegs. He returned to the rear of the van and sat.

"Man, we never had to go through this sort of thing before," the driver commented with a sneer.

"Just routine," one of the FB Agents said and concluded, "you're okay and can proceed."

"Gee, thank you," the driver said sarcastically.

—

"Hey Ian, what's your twenty?" Chalmers spoke into his cell phone.

"We're just coming off the Bay Bridge. Where are you?" Ian replied.

"I'm here at the Security Personnel Entrance at Candlestick Park with Dinosa and Chad waiting for you. We have your security badges," Chalmers said.

"We'll meet you there in fifteen," Ian said hanging up.

"God, I hope Chad knows what he's doing," Dinosa said, pacing back and forth in front of the security gate.

She continued, "Valerie Kane is the kick off speaker tonight and she's going to announce her candidacy for Mayor. The woman is a masochist, I swear to God. We all might be dead by tomorrow."

"Mary, I'm proud of you. I believe that's the first time I've heard you put three or four sentences together without using vulgarity," Chalmers said with chuckle, "What, are you trying to get right with your maker?"

"Eat me, Chalmers. There, is that better?"

Chad said, "If you wanted to plant a dirty bomb in this stadium how would you get it in and where would you put it? We've practically torn the stage apart, we've thoroughly checked and searched the stands, press boxes and mezzanine level VIP suites and the concession stands and we've turned up nothing suspicious. We even checked out the player's locker rooms and cafeteria. We've inspected every square inch of this place with bomb detecting devices and bomb sniffing dogs."

"Hmm," Chalmers mused, "How do the concession supplies enter the grounds and where are they stored?"

Carbohal pulled an I-Pod from his back pack and squatted down. Chalmers and Dinosa leaned over to observe as Chad brought up an architectural drawing of the stadium and surrounding grounds.

Pointing at an exit road off the Bay Shore Freeway Ball Park exit, Carbohal said, "Delivery vehicles are instructed to take this exit which is designated for them only. It continues along here to an inspection station here at the southeast side of the stadium. After being inspected they continue here to a loading dock where the goods are unloaded and either hand trucked or forklifted to a series of three cargo elevators located here in this bay. From there they're taken either one level down to a dry goods area or two levels down to a cold storage locker. This morning we went through the storage areas with a fine tooth comb."

"Since you inspected these areas this morning, are any of the goods inspected after they've passed through this security check point?" Chalmers asked, pointing at the drawing.

Chad scratched his head, looked quizzically at Chalmers and simply answered, "No."

Chalmers handed one of the security guards the security badges for Ian, Grant and Jesse and said. "Would you give these to them when they arrive and direct them to the loading dock?"

Chad was already on his radio saying, "Marley, meet me with your team at the cargo elevators."

Dinosa and Chalmers crowded onto a golf cart and with Carbohal driving they sped off down a paved path and around to the loading dock. When they arrived and were standing at the elevator, Carbohal said, "Beer kegs. The explosives and dirty bombs are in beer kegs."

As they waited for the elevator, the Explosive Detection team consisting of four men arrived. One man led the group who were equipped with a German Sheppard on a leash and a mobile ultrasound device.

Chalmers was on his mobile phone, "Ian what's your ETA?"

"Shit, Chuck we're stuck in traffic at a crawl! We're on Third Street and we can see the stadium. I'm not sure, but maybe fifteen minutes," Ian replied.

"We may have found the bomb. I suggest you pull over and park and I'll keep you posted," Chalmers said.

"Roger."

The elevator arrived and the group entered and Chad pressed the B2 button. As they slowly descended the two Budweiser delivery men exited from the adjacent elevator onto the loading dock level above.

Walking across the bay toward their truck, the smaller man said, "It's in God's hands now."

When the elevator doors opened at level B2, Chalmers and the others were greeted by another security guard holding a clip board and standing in front of the cold storage locker door.

Carbohal took the clip board from the guard and read the supply log in record and said, "It looks like there've been three deliveries since we inspected this area this morning. Twenty five kegs of Corona Beer, a load of boxed goods from Ghirardelli Deli Meats and fifty kegs of Budweiser Beer."

He opened the locker door and the team was greeted by a rush of cold air as they entered the bay. It appeared each supplier had a designated area to store their goods. Aisles of racks lined the east wall filled with boxes of bread, meats, vegetables and other consumables. The north end of the bay contained the soda pop and other nonalcoholic beverages. Beer kegs, separated by brand covered the west wall and extended out to the center of the bay.

"Okay Marley, let's be very careful with this inspection. We believe there is a good chance one or more of these kegs are filled with explosives ad rigged to blow. They could have a secondary tilt ignition switch, savvy?"

Marley returned a facetious 'dah' look to remind Chad that he was a former bomb disposal specialist with the Army Rangers and had been on several previous combat operations with him.

"Just show us where to start," Marley replied.

Chad looked down at the clip board and said, "Let's start with the last delivery, these Budweiser kegs."

Marley removed his boots and motioned to his partner who held the mobile ultrasound device to do the same. He removed an I-Pod from his satchel and gingerly crawled up on top of a keg.

"Come on up, Filly, and be careful. We'll start at the back row and work forward. If I was going to plant a bomb, I'd put it in the most remote area," he waved at Bill Fillmore, another former Army Ranger he had served with.

"If you spot anything, sing out," he added.

They carefully stepped from one keg to another until they had reached the back row and far corner of the Budweiser stash.

"Freeze," Marley said calmly.

"We found one," he yelled back at the others and then added, "Holy shit! It's wired to another and...Christ, another!"

He had spotted a small switch with a red LED lamp lit, mounted on top of the far corner keg. Peering down its' side about half way, three wires connected the key to the one next to it and three wires from that key connected it to the adjacent one.

"Scan this one," Carbohal said, as he turned on his I-Pod.

Fillmore slowly moved the ultrasound probe over the first key keg and an image started appearing on Chad's I-Pod.

"Okay, this is the master and I'm gonna guess the other two are auxiliary slaves," Marley said and added, "Let's scan them."

"What's it look like?" Chad called anxiously.

"This has got to be it. I'll have to analyze the scanned images to know for sure, but I think we've got one master full of some kind of explosive and the other two contain an explosive liquid material and it looks like your cobalt pellets. At any rate, I'd evacuate the stadium and surrounding area." Marley replied.

Carbohal depressed the send button on his radio and said, "All teams, commence evacuation drill now. Get everybody out of the stadium and clear of the parking lot. Secure perimeter and allow no one in."

"What time does the log indicate the Budweiser delivery was made?" Chalmers asked.

Chad checked the clip board and say, "Jesus Christ, they had to be leaving about the same time we got here."

Chalmers retrieved his cell phone from his pocket and said, "Shit, there's no signal down here. Come on Mary, let's get upstairs."

They found the stairwell and covered the steps two at a time as they raced up. When they exited the stairs on the ground floor Chalmers said, "Mary, get a hold of SFPD and have them issue an APB to all Bay Area law enforcement agencies to stop any Budweiser truck and detain the occupants and get someone to the local Budweiser distribution center and secure it."

Chalmers already had his phone out and speed dialed Ian.

"Ian, we've found the bomb, or I should say bombs. They're contained in Budweiser kegs in the cold storage area. Chad's bomb disposal people are attempting to disarm them now. We believe the delivery truck just left the stadium grounds and an APB has been issued.

"I suggest you monitor the police scanner and proceed to the point where the truck is stopped."

"Jesus Chuck, a Budweiser truck just passed us going north on Third Street." Ian exclaimed and as he hit the van's accelerator and spun a U-turn he added, "We're on them!"

"Ian, keep this line open and keep us apprised of your location. Dinosa is in contact with SFPD and will relay the information," Chalmers said.

Ian handed his phone to a bewildered Jesse sitting in the passenger seat and said, "Put this on speaker. We're after the Budweiser truck that just passed us not more than a minute ago."

The northbound traffic was considerably lighter and Ian weaved in and out of the three lanes. As they approached a traffic light and intersection the green light was in their favor. Ian slowed and when Jesse pointed left and yelled, "There it is!" Ian swung the van into oncoming traffic narrowly missing several cars going in the opposite direction and made the turn.

"He's down a couple of blocks and it looks like he's making another left on the Bay Shore Boulevard," Jesse exclaimed.

The van was a block behind the delivery truck and barely made the left turn green arrow as Ian swung wide and squealed around the corner. He slowed and kept a safe distance from the truck.

"Chuck, we're now southbound on Bay Shore Boulevard, but let's keep that between us. They may lead us to the others," Ian said loud enough for his phone to pick up.

"Not a bad idea," Chalmers replied and grabbing Dinosa by the arm he motioned for her to hang up her phone.

"Chief, I gotta go, but I'll be in touch," Dinosa said into her phone and hung up.

With Dinosa in tow, Chalmers ran and jumped into the gold cart and cried into his phone, "Ian, keep us informed of your twenty, Mary and I are on our way."

As they sped down the frontage road toward the parking lot and his car, Dinosa asked, "What the hell is going on?"

Chalmers filled her in and by the time they were in his car and speeding across the parking lot Mary already had her forty caliper semi-automatic pistol out and checking it was locked and loaded.

—

PART V

THE RESURRECTION

"Up from the grave he arose; with a mighty triumph oe'r his foes; he arose a victor form the dark domain…" Lyrics from the spiritual, 'Up from the Grave He Arose'.

CHAPTER TWENTY

The barrels surrounding the three keg bombs had been removed creating a clear path. Chad and Marley were squatted over the I-Pod that was now piggy backed to a lap top computer.

"The timer and detonator are pretty simple and straight forward. The interconnecting three wires simply receive a signal that detonates the explosive. One of the three wires is a fail safe return and if cut first it will tell the mother board that will by-pass the timer and send all her babies to heaven," Marley said.

"Why Marley, I never knew you were religious?" Chad chuckled nervously.

"We were told man years ago, 'there are no atheists in a fox hole'," Marley smiled.

"How do we know which two wires to cut first?" Chad asked, hoping for a confident answer.

"We don't," Marley replied.

Chad's jaw dropped, but Marley quickly replied, "But not to worry."

He retrieved a tool from his bag that Chad had never seen before. Holding it up he said, "We call this GiGi, or God's Guillotine. It's a spring loaded wire cutter. We set the spring, gently arrange the wires parallel on this little platform, hit this here little switch and voila, off with their heads all at the same time."

"Jesus Marley, won't the blade itself complete the circuit?" Carbohal questioned.

"Nope, it's a nonconductive ceramic blade. If..."

"Please don't use that word," Chad pleaded.

"You're absolutely right. When we've eliminated the detonator's source, we can safely remove the two kegs that contain the dirty material. That'll leave just me and this baby here," Marley said reaching over and gently patting the beer keg.

"Don't you think it'd be wise if we donned bomb suits before we continue?" Chad asked.

Marley chuckled and said, "That would be a waste of the tax-payer's money. From the density numbers calculated by our little ultrasound unit, I'm guessing this tank is filled with NGX. That was an explosive that was still in the development stage when I was in the army. It's a mixture of nitroglycerine and a highly classified, but I was told a very stable chemical. It was said it would take only a few ounces of this shit to bring down the Empire State Building. Which reminds me, has the mile wide evacuation been completed yet?"

"No, they said it would take another hour or so. In the meantime, if you think it's safe, let's diffuse these two dirty kegs and get them the hell out of here."

"Right on, Leon," Marley replied with a smirk.

—

"We just turned west onto Industrial Boulevard," Chalmers heard Ian say as he and Dinosa sped south on Bay Shore Boulevard in pursuit of their three comrades.

"We're about two and a half miles behind them," Dinosa said, monitoring the on board GPS.

Ian stayed well behind the Budweiser Delivery truck as they wound through the light industrial park consisting of mostly storage facility warehouses. They watched the truck slow down and make a wide turn and enter an alley between two warehouses. They drove by and noticed a realtor's 'For Lease' sign posted in the front window of the two buildings and saw the delivery truck swing around the rear of the left side building and disappear. Ian pulled over to the curb, parked and the three men got out.

Most of the surrounding buildings were vacant and reminded Ian of the sad economical state his country now found itself. The feeble and usually self-serving attempts by the White House and the Congress to pull the country out of the financial depression had failed miserably and actually contributed to the lackluster and some would say phony recovery.

"Okay," Ian started, "Is everybody locked and loaded?"

Each man had donned a double shoulder harness holster and checked that both of their forty caliber handgun clips were loaded and the weapons chambered.

"What's the plan?" Grant asked.

"Let's do a little recon first. There's only a single window and door on the frontage here. If this is a typical warehouse behind that door is probably a small office area and the rest of the building will be an open bay for storage. We'll wait here for Chalmers and Dinosa. They can block the alley with their vehicle and cover that door.

"The three of us will then proceed to the rear of the warehouse on foot and see if we can secure the building and wait for back up and see what develops." Ian said.

Dinosa and Chalmers pulled up and parked behind the van. As Chalmers exited the driver's side Ian approached the two and filled them in on the plan. He ended the briefing by saying, "If anybody comes out of that door without their hands up, I'd shoot and ask questions later."

When the group was together, Dinosa said, "Okay guys, we want to take these guys alive, believe it or not. Hopefully a negotiation team will be here soon and we can talk them out, but if the shit starts, let's make sure we all walk away from this."

Everyone nodded in agreement and as Ian, Jesse and Grant started walking in single file next to the building and down the alley, Chalmers pulled the van around and blocked the alley's exit.

—

Members of the bomb disposal team had loaded the two kegs filled with the nuclear waste material onto a palette and were prepared to roll them away with a palette jack to the awaiting bomb disposal vehicle located at the loading dock two stories above.

"Chad, you better join them. I can handle it from here," Marley said as a matter of fact.

"Nah, you ain't getting off that easy. Besides, you might be able to use me and remember, no one left behind," Chad winked.

"Suit yourself, but what the hell. If this thing goes off, we won't feel a thing. We'll be a mass of vaporized atoms in about one nanosecond."

Chad's radio cackled and said, "The kegs and men are clear."

Chad replied, "Roger," and then turned to Marley and said, "Let's do this."

Marley removed a hex headed drive tool from his tool pouch and began loosening the bolt of the band car buckle that secured the keg's lid to the barrel. Once this was accomplished, he gently unsnapped the car buckle and removed the band.

"Hmm, so far so good," Marley remarked. "Okay, I'm gonna lift this lid and I need you to take two of those pieces of one-byes and place them on either side of the lid so I can rest it on them and then take a looksee at what we have."

Chad picked up two pieces from a stack of one by two, by twelve inch sticks and moved closer to the keg. Marley started to slowly lift the lid.

Marley was right about one thing. Neither man felt a thing as the NCX compound exploded in a thunderous and devastating inferno.

Three miles away at the warehouse, approaching sirens could be heard when the ground shook and a distant roar echoed off the warehouse walls. A huge smoke cloud could be seen rising from the northern horizon and as it ascended, the brisk afternoon breeze moved it slowly in a southeastern direction.

"Let's keep focused, people. Sounds like the police will be here any moment." Ian said into his ear phone.

He and Jesse were stationed on either side of the large roll up door at the rear of the warehouse and Grant had stationed himself in a position to cover the loading dock and back man door.

Suddenly the roll up door started to rise. Both Ian and Jesse crouched and lowered their weapons. The door opened high enough to expose the man pulling the door's lift chain and the Humvee pointed in their direction about ten meters behind him.

Ian yelled, "Freeze, let me see your hands!"

The man let go of the chain and reached for a pistol tucked in his pants. Ian shot twice and the man stumbled and fell. The Humvee's motor roared and then lurched forward and stopped abruptly.

Grant had moved from his previous position and now stood squarely in the middle of the doorway with both of his pistols out and leveled at the Humvee. He was flanked on either side by Ian and Jesse with their weapons aimed at the same target. The tinted windows didn't allow them to see the vehicle's occupants.

"Turn off the ignition and exit the vehicle with your hands out, now!" Ian bellowed.

"I got the left, Jesse you got the right and Grant you got the driver," Ian said to his companions.

Suddenly the Humvee lurched forward toward the three men and they opened fire. The vehicle's front windshield shattered and bullet holes pierced the hood as it veered to the left and rammed into the frame of the roll up door.

Two men exited the opposite side of the Humvee and returned fire with fully automatic rifles. Ian took cover between the crumpled grill of the Humvee and the roll up door frame but didn't have a shot and felt helpless as he watched Grant charge the vehicle, take a round and stumble to the floor.

Jesse had taken a position behind the opposite side of the roll up door frame and was returning fire. Ian dropped to his belly hoping he could at least get a foot shot from beneath the vehicle, but the damaged bumper and grill blocked his view.

During a moments lull in the shooting the clanging of boots on metal steps could be heard and a man's voice yell, "Cover me!"

"He's going to the roof!" Ian yelled at Jesse.

"I know, but I don't have a shot," Jesse replied in a shout.

As the other man opened fire once again, Jesse dropped to his belly and started shooting blindly into the darkness underneath the Humvee. The automatic fire suddenly ceased and a man groaning in pain was all that could be heard.

"Let's go, go!" Ian yelled and he climbed over the Humvees hood. A man laid writhing and groaning on the cold concrete floor before him, his rifle laying several feet from his feet. Jesse appeared from the rear of the vehicle and picked up the weapon.

The man on the ground quit moaning and moving and lay now quietly in a pool of blood. Ian knelt down and checked his carotid artery for a pulse. He looked up at Jesse and shook his head. Inside the Humvee a bloody man lay dead, slumped over the steering wheel.

"Hey, a little help over here, if it's not too much to ask?"

Their hearts leapt with joy as both men realized it was the voice of Grant. They ran around the Humvee and up to their fallen comrade who was sitting up and tightening his belt around his right leg stemming the blood loss from a wound. He was also bleeding profusely from what had been his right ear.

"Jesus Christ, why am I the only one that gets shot in these things?" Grant complained.

Jesse had removed his shirt and was wrapping Grant's head with it. He chuckled and replied, "You're a bigger target than me and you obviously have bigger ears, or should I say ear."

"Stay here and tend to Grant," Ian said and he turned and ran to the spiral staircase that led to the roof and scurried up. When he reached the platform exit door to the roof he paused, checked and reloaded one of his pistols, pushed the door open and stepped back.

Automatic gun fire greeted and blew holes through the door, but suddenly the shooting stopped and Ian could hear metallic clicking he had heard many times before. It was the sound of a jammed weapon. Cautiously he stepped out and from behind the door.

He found himself facing what he believed to be the incarnation of the Devil. Fire blazed from the man's eyes set sunken below black bushy brows on a wrinkled face framed by wild gray hair and an unkempt white beard. Ian realized he was staring into the eyes of pure evil.

The man was peering over Ian's should and his thin chapped lips broke into a wide wicked grin. "Armageddon has begun," he sneered.

Ian glanced to the north and saw the large black cloud that now obscured the Bay Bridge and the East Bay shoreline. When he looked back at the Devil he saw the man had a small capsule between his thumb and forefinger and was moving it toward his mouth. Ian took aim and fired.

The man's eyes widened in amazement and horror as he watched his capsule, thumb and forefinger disappear and then shut them with a wince as his own blood sprayed his face.

Ian walked casually over to the man and growled, "I don't know about Armageddon, but I do know your Hell is just beginning, pal."

—

CHAPTER TWENTY-ONE

Beneath the bold headline; '**BOMB LEVELS HALF OF CANDLESTICK PARK AND ROCKS PARTS OF SOUTH CITY**,**'** in that evening's special edition of the San Francisco Tribune and filling the remainder of the front page was an aerial photograph of the ball park still smoldering from that afternoon's explosion.

The article that followed on the ensuing pages began; *The Armageddon promised recently by the 'Great White Nation' came to pass in our City earlier today, but fate and the heroics of two men proved the threat was not a God inspired act. What could have been the worst nuclear disaster in the history of the world was averted...*

The article went on to relate the fact that the bomb had been detected and dirty nuclear waste was successfully removed from the scene and was on its' way to a nuclear waste disposal area in New Mexico when the bomb, still located inside the stadium was accidently detonated while two members of a private contractor's bomb disposal team attempted to disarm it. The names of the two heroes had not been released, pending the notification of the next of kin.

The stadium and surrounding neighborhoods had been previously and successfully evacuated and other than some shattered windows, no other structural damage or human casualties resulted.

A related story starting on page three under the headline **'SUSPECTED GWN LEADER CAPTURED'**, reported the story surrounding the capture of the wounded suspect, Frank Wilbur Johnson, a.k.a. 'Joshua', and the discovery of three dead suspected friends of Johnson and fellow GWN members at a vacant warehouse in South San Francisco. Identification of the dead men was unknown at the time of publication, but Johnson was believed to be originally from Arkansas and had family living in the Bay Area and may have aided and abetted the cult.

Mr. Johnson had been taken to an undisclosed location and authorities refused to release details of the capture except to say it was the result of an investigation by the FBI and local police authorities.

—

Dinosa, Ian and Chalmers all stood up and waved Valerie Kane over to their table as she entered 'Lefty's Tavern'. Mary embraced Val with a long hug and whispered, 'Val, I'm so sorry."

The four mourners took a seat and Ian broke the long silence, lifting his beer mug and saying somberly, "Here's to our good friend and fellow warrior, Chad Carbohal, may you rest in peace."

Valerie followed saying, "And here's to all of you, his fellow warriors, whose actions have made a difference."

The End...?

EPILOGUE

"I can't help but think that four short years ago it took the acts of a deranged, diabolical individual to bring us together," Solomon Goldsmith remarked. as he sat in a lounge chair on the deck of his Cliff House home overlooking the Pacific Ocean and sharing the view of a beautiful sunset with his friends George Armstrong and Sean O'Farrell.

"Yes," Armstrong sighed, "and I believe they all would have agreed to and supported our decisions since."

O'Farrell chuckled and said, "Hell, my wife Louan would have insisted on it."

Goldsmith poured a splash of brandy in his and his guests snifters, lifted his glass and said, "Here's to Louan, Margaret and Cheryl."

—

"Now don't look, don't peek," Chalmers chided Colleen as he helped his wife with her hands covering her eyes down the steps from their front porch.

Pointing her towards the drive way he said "Okay, you can look."

Colleen removed her hands and blinked in confusion, "Ah, ah?" she stammered looking up at her husband.

"I figured we could use it to tour the country until we find a place where we'd like to retire. You're going to love it. It has a full kitchen and bathroom and a king sized bed," Chalmers cried excitingly.

They stood in front of a deluxe thirty-five foot motor home encircled with a wide red ribbon and a bow on the top.

Colleen took a step back from him and said, "Charles Raymond Chalmers, are you serious? Are we really going to retire?"

"Yep," he replied.

She leapt into his arms and cried, "Oh Chuck, its' perfect!"

Jennifer stood behind them on the porch and beamed.

—

"Wow, what a day, hell, what a year," Bernard Rusk said slumped in the chair across the desk from Valerie Kane in her Federal Building office.

"You said it," Kane said, pouring a shot of Makers Mark bourbon into two glasses and handing one to him.

She went on, "This is a resilient City and we'll get over today. Candlestick Park was scheduled for demolition next month anyway so any scheduled events will have to be postponed or their venue changed, including the GAALFI event this weekend. But I am worried for our Country, Bernie. What's going to happen?"

"Well, I don't believe our Country has faced a bigger challenge since the Civil War, but we managed to get through it and I have faith we'll survive this. My sources say our Attorney General and other Benjamin insiders and covert supporters have fled the country to one of the rogue Islamic nations and have vowed to continue their 'crusade' against the United States.

"In light of the overwhelming support of Congress to impeach and convict him, President Benjamin will resign tomorrow morning. Virtually every one of his Cabinet Heads has been indicted and those who have not joined their comrades in hiding are being arrested as we speak.

"Besides brave people like Corky Burmeister, people are crawling out of the woodwork to whistle blow on their bosses. Although we had a good idea, the corruption in this Administration goes deeper than even we believed.

"Some die hard Benjamin supporters will cause some unrest and perhaps even some minor rioting, but most of the African American community and their honest leaders are behind us," Rusk remarked.

"Although Vice President Brown is not the brightest bulb in the package, he's a loyal American and not a Benjamin insider and that should make the transition less traumatic," he concluded.

"You know Bernie, when I headed up the Justice Department investigation of the drug cartels and government corruption over a year ago, I had no idea it would eventually lead to the President. Why didn't you tell me, considering how high and widespread the corruption was, how we were so successful then?"

"That information is based on a need to know basis," Rusk said with a smile and continued, "I'd like to convince you to join the flock and become one of those 'need to know' people."

Leaning forward, Kane replied, "I'm all ears."

—

"If you're sitting on this side of him, the big lug can't hear a word your saying," Jesse said, addressing Nancy Cromwell who was seated to his right a large table in the Obsidian Lodge, now closed for the season.

"Did you know, his momma wears combat boots," Jesse chuckled.

Grant sitting on his other side with a bandaged right ear, turned to a surprised Jesse and in mock anger hollered, "That's because your momma's boots are too small!"

The 'Justice Foundation' team, gathered around the table roared with laughter. When it subsided, Ian excused himself to go to the restroom.

Mary Dinosa's cell phone rang and retrieving it from her bag she turned her back from the table and answered, "Dinosa here."

"Knowing how you love romantic telephone conversation," a familiar voice said, "Mary Florence Dinosa…"

She felt a tap on her shoulder and turned to find a kneeling Ian O'Farrell holding an open box containing a sparkling diamond wedding ring.

"…Will you marry me?"

—

Snoopy and Grub sat snuggled on the love seat swing on the lanai of their rental beach cottage watching the sun set in Princeville, Kauai, Hawaii. It was their favorite island resort and they were happy to share it on their second wedding anniversary.

Grub had his arm draped over Snoop's shoulder and his other hand gently massaged her belly bump.

"You know Daniel, with the baby coming and all, I think we should start addressing each other by our real first names," Snoopy said.

"If you insist, Belinda," Grub replied.

"Speaking of names, have you any thoughts about a name for junior?" she asked.

"Pig Pen, of course," Grub replied seriously.

"Oh Grub, you're so incorrigible."

—

Would you like to see your manuscript become a book?

If you are interested in becoming a PublishAmerica author, please submit your manuscript for possible publication to us at:

mybook@publishamerica.com

You may also mail in your manuscript to:

**PublishAmerica
PO Box 151
Frederick, MD 21705**

www.publishamerica.com

CPSIA information can be obtained at www.ICGtesting.com
Printed in the USA
BVOW07s1440290913

332343BV00001B/41/P